REX STOUT, the creator of Nero Wolfe, was born in Noblesville, Indiana, in 1886, the sixth of nine children of John and Lucetta Todhunter Stout, both Quakers. Shortly after his birth, the family moved to Wakarusa, Kansas. He was educated in a country school, but, by the age of nine, was recognized throughout the state as a prodigy in arithmetic. Mr. Stout briefly attended the University of Kansas, but left to enlist in the Navy, and spent the next two years as a warrant officer on board President Theodore Roosevelt's yacht. When he left the Navy in 1908, Rex Stout began to write free-lance articles, worked as a sightseeing guide and as an itinerant bookkeeper. Later he devised and implemented a school banking system which was installed in four hundred cities and towns throughout the country. In 1927 Mr. Stout retired from the world of finance and, with the proceeds of his banking scheme, left for Paris to write serious fiction. He wrote three novels that received favorable reviews before turning to detective fiction. His first Nero Wolfe novel, *Fer-de-Lance*, appeared in 1934. It was followed by many others, among them *Too Many Cooks*, *The Silent Speaker*, *If Death Ever Slept*, *The Doorbell Rang*, and *Please Pass the Guilt*, which established Nero Wolfe as a leading character on a par with Erle Stanley Gardner's famous protagonist, Perry Mason. During World War II, Rex Stout waged a personal campaign against Nazism as chairman of the War Writers' Board, master of ceremonies of the radio program "Speaking of Liberty," and as a member of several national committees. After the war, he turned his attention to mobilizing public opinion against the wartime use of thermonuclear devices, was an active leader in the Authors' Guild, and resumed writing his Nero Wolfe novels. Rex Stout died in 1975 at the age of eighty-nine. A month before his death, he published his seventy-second Nero Wolfe mystery, *A Family Affair*. Ten years later, a seventy-third Nero Wolfe mystery was discovered and published in *Death Times Three*.

The Rex Stout Library

Fer-de-Lance
The League of Frightened Men
The Rubber Band
The Red Box
Too Many Cooks
Some Buried Caesar
Over My Dead Body
Where There's a Will
Black Orchids
Not Quite Dead Enough
The Silent Speaker
Too Many Women
And Be a Villain
The Second Confession
Trouble in Triplicate
In the Best Families
Three Doors to Death
Murder by the Book
Curtains for Three
Prisoner's Base
Triple Jeopardy
The Golden Spiders
The Black Mountain

Three Men Out
Before Midnight
Might As Well Be Dead
Three Witnesses
If Death Ever Slept
Three for the Chair
Champagne for One
And Four to Go
Plot It Yourself
Too Many Clients
Three at Wolfe's Door
The Final Deduction
Gambit
Homicide Trinity
The Mother Hunt
A Right to Die
Trio for Blunt Instruments
The Doorbell Rang
Death of a Doxy
The Father Hunt
Death of a Dude
Please Pass the Guilt
A Family Affair
Death Times Three

REX STOUT

Not Quite Dead Enough

*Introduction
by John Lutz*

BANTAM BOOKS

NEW YORK • TORONTO • LONDON • SYDNEY • AUCKLAND

A NERO WOLFE
MYSTERY

This book is fiction. No resemblance is intended
between any character herein and any person,
living or dead; any such resemblance is
purely coincidental.

NOT QUITE DEAD ENOUGH
*A Bantam Crime Line Book / published by arrangement with
the author*
PUBLISHING HISTORY
Farrar & Rinehart edition published September 1944
Bantam edition / October 1982
Bantam reissue / October 1992

CRIME LINE *and the portrayal of a boxed "cl" are trademarks of Bantam Books,
a division of Random House, Inc.*

All rights reserved.
Copyright © 1942, 1944 by Rex Stout.
Introduction copyright © 1992 by John Lutz.
Cover art copyright © 1992 by Tom Hallman.
*No part of this book may be reproduced or transmitted in any
form or by any means, electronic or mechanical, including
photocopying, recording, or by any information storage and
retrieval system, without permission in writing from the publisher.
For information address: Bantam Books.*

ISBN 978-0-553-26109-7

Published simultaneously in the United States and Canada

*Bantam Books are published by Bantam Books, a division of Random
House, Inc. Its trademark, consisting of the words "Bantam Books" and
the portrayal of a rooster, is Registered in U.S. Patent and Trademark
Office and in other countries. Marca Registrada, Bantam Books, New
York, New York.*

PRINTED IN THE UNITED STATES OF AMERICA

OPM   20 19 18 17 16 15 14 13

Contents

1
Not Quite Dead Enough
page 1

2
Booby Trap
page 93

Introduction

Archie's in the army.

He's Major Archie Goodwin now, and the urbane but reclusive three-hundred-pound master detective Nero Wolfe is emerging from his West 35th Street brownstone with regularity to train with his chef, Fritz Brenner, for some future combat envisioned by Wolfe.

When Major Goodwin calls at the venerable brownstone, he's told that Wolfe and Brenner are out walking, as they are every morning these days, in an effort to toughen themselves and to sweat some weight off the corpulent Wolfe. They are by the river, where, a shocked Archie is told, Wolfe "obtained permission from the authorities to train on a pier because the boys on the street ridicule him."

When Wolfe and Fritz return Archie ruefully observes them eating an unappetizing breakfast of prunes, lettuce, and tomatoes. The regimen seems to be working, at least in the mind of Wolfe, and the astounded Archie is told that next week the two intend to begin running.

But beyond these strange circumstances, not much has changed in the universe of Nero Wolfe and Archie

Goodwin. The war years didn't slow the remarkable Rex Stout's prolificity or ingenuity. Quite the contrary. The patriotic Stout was the host of three radio programs during the war, and served as chairman of the War Writers' Board. He was also president of Friends of Democracy, 1941–51, the Authors' Guild, 1943–45, and the Society for the Prevention of World War III, 1943–46. When it came to serving his country, both during and after World War II, this amazing author was busier than the marines. Yet somehow during the war years he found the time and talent to create four novels, *The Broken Vase*, *Alphabet Hicks*, *Black Orchids*, and *Not Quite Dead Enough*.

In the latter, the hugely overweight Wolfe might be training for physical rough stuff, but Archie, assigned by the army to obtain Wolfe's help, realizes it's Wolfe's brain and not brawn that would best serve the cause. So, after some neat maneuvering by the shrewd and supremely competent Archie, the two complementary characters are at it as always in *Not Quite Dead Enough*, Wolfe the lazy, unparalleled genius in his comfortable West Side brownstone, Archie the affable, energetic, and resourceful legman working the streets of Manhattan and environs.

The familiar cast of satellite characters also appears. There are daring and dangerous Lily Rowan, still trying and sometimes succeeding in manipulating Archie by his heartstrings, and the intrepid, antagonistic, and usually one-step-behind Inspector Cramer, who isn't at all agreeable to Wolfe and Archie meddling in New York Police business, especially if that business is a homicide investigation.

This investigation is already complicated by the oddball tenants of an apartment building with a rooftop pigeon coop, folks described by even the worldly and tolerant Archie as "the goofy assortment of specimens." Inspector Cramer would much rather that Wolfe and Archie weren't part of the mix.

While the mood and tempo of *Not Quite Dead Enough* is, I am happy to report, representative of the Wolfe body of work, and it is a book that exists despite the war rather than because of it, the novel also provides some interesting glimpses into New York life and attitudes in the tumultuous early forties. Who better as a tour guide for this time travel to the war years than the masterful, patriotic, and indefatigable Rex Stout, through his wonderful creations Wolfe and Archie?

All of the Nero Wolfe novels are cleverly and tightly plotted, smooth, stylish, and generously peppered with wit and insight. Wolfe and his live-in confidential assistant Archie are in many ways direct opposites: Wolfe is essentially cerebral, engaging in little physical activity and absorbed in his hobbies of orchid growing, reading, eating fine food prepared by Fritz, and drinking (beer and more beer). And, of course, occasionally solving crimes. Archie has a sharp and retentive mind, but he's more the physical type, needing to roam and be among the common man and woman in bustling and raucous New York, while Wolfe needs to spend hours alone in his office or his plant rooms among quiet, exotic orchids. The obese Wolfe is in his fifties, and the trim and handsome Archie is in his thirties, causing at times a clash of generations as well as one of personalities. But wry observations and acidic remarks aside, the two have affection and respect for each other, personally and professionally.

I've long been an avid fan of Rex Stout's Nero Wolfe novels. I admire Stout's fascinating characters, his innovative plots, the subtle but complete and totally believable world he created. He made it seem easy, and I know it isn't.

The New York of Nero Wolfe and Archie Goodwin still exists between the covers of Stout's books, waiting for us to enter. For that we should be grateful, because it's a place worth visiting, where calm reasoning (Wolfe) and dogged determination and physical energy (Archie) ultimately bring desired results. Though it's a delicate balance to be sure, Stout's New York is a city where order still outweighs chaos, while perhaps in the New York of the nineties it's become the other way around.

Not Quite Dead Enough is quintessential Nero Wolfe. The fact that it is set on the World War II home front only adds to its solid sense of place. Stout skillfully weaves us into that not-so-long-ago and still familiar prenuclear era that was governed by simple, important principles and the obvious necessity of national survival.

It is in this place and time that Wolfe and Archie must cope with one of the most ancient, persistent, and horrible problems plaguing the human race—not war, but murder. Despite their opposing outlooks and their sometimes acerbic banter, these two very different men, united in a common purpose, know and understand each other well. And they know that as a team they are the best.

Millions of readers over six decades have concurred. I think you'll agree with their assessment.

—John Lutz

Not Quite
Dead Enough

Chapter 1

We swooped down and hit the concrete alongside the Potomac at 1:20 p.m. on a raw Monday in early March.

I didn't know whether I would be staying in Washington or hopping a plane for Detroit or Africa, so I checked my bags at the parcel room at the airport and went out front and flagged a taxi. For twenty minutes I sat back and watched the driver fight his way through two million government employees, in uniforms and in civies, on wheels and on foot, and for another twenty minutes, after entering a building, I showed credentials and waited and let myself be led through corridors, and finally was ushered into a big room with a big desk.

It was the first time I had ever seen the top mackaroo of United States Army Intelligence. He was in uniform and had two chins and a pair of eyes that wasted neither time nor space. I was perfectly willing to shake hands, but he just said to sit down, glanced at a paper on top of a pile and told me in a dry brittle voice that my name was Archie Goodwin.

I nodded noncommittally. For all I knew, it was a military secret.

He inquired acidly, "What the hell is the matter with Nero Wolfe?"

"Search me, sir. Why, is he sick?"

"You worked for him for ten years. As his chief assistant in the detective business. Didn't you?"

"All of that. Yes, sir. But I never found out what was the matter with him. However, if you want some good guesses—"

"You seem to have done pretty well with that mess down in Georgia, Major Goodwin."

"Much obliged, sir. Speaking of Nero Wolfe—"

"I am about to." He shoved the papers aside. "That's why I sent for you. Is he crazy?"

"That's one theory." I looked judicious and crossed my legs, remembered who I was now, and uncrossed them. "He's a great man, I grant that, but you know what it was that made the Australian wild dog so wild. Assistant is not the word for it. I was a combination accelerator and brake. I may mention that my pay was roughly three times what it is at the moment. Of course if I were made a colonel—"

"How long have you been a major?"

"Three days."

He pronounced a certain word, just one word, very snappy.

"Yes, sir," I said.

He nodded curtly, to signify that that was settled for good, and went on. "We need Nero Wolfe. Not necessarily in uniform, but we need him. I don't know whether he deserves his reputation—"

"He does," I declared. "I hate to admit it, but he does."

"Very well. That seems to be the prevailing opinion. And we need him, and we've tried to get him. He has been seen by Captain Cross and by Colonel Ryder, and he refused to call on General Fife. I have a report here—"

"They handled him wrong." I grinned. "He wouldn't call on the King of China even if there was one. I doubt if he's been outdoors since I left, two months ago. The only thing he has got is brains, and the only way to go is to take things to him: facts, problems, people—"

The mackaroo was shaking his head impatiently. "We tried to. Colonel Ryder went to try to get him to work on a certain matter of great importance, and he flatly refused. He's no fascist or appeaser, according to his record. What's wrong with him?"

"Nothing sir. Nothing like that. He's probably in a bad mood. His moods never are anything to brag about, and of course he's dejected because I'm not there. But the main thing is they don't know how to handle him."

"Do you know how to handle him?"

"Yes, sir."

"Then go and do it. We want him on a day basis under Schedule 34H. We want him immediately and urgently on a matter that Colonel Ryder went to him about. Nobody has even been able to make a start on it. How long will it take you?"

"I couldn't say. It all depends." I stood up with my heels together. "An hour, a day, a week, two weeks. I'll have to live in his house with him as I always did. The best time to work on him is late at night."

"Very well. On your arrival, report to Colonel Ryder at Governor's Island by telephone, report progress to him, and tell him when you are ready for him to see Mr. Wolfe." He got up and offered me a hand, and I took it. "And don't waste any time."

In another room downstairs I found they had got me a priority for a seat on the three o'clock plane for New York, and a taxi got me to the airport just in time to weigh my luggage through and make a run for it.

Chapter 2

All the seats were taken but one, the outside of a double near the front, and I nodded down at the occupant of the seat next to the window, a man with spectacles and a tired face, stuffed my hat and coat on the shelf, and lowered myself. In another minute we were taxiing down the runway, turning, vibrating, rolling, picking it up, and in the air. Just as I unfastened my seat belt, dainty female fingers gripped the seat arm, a female figure stopped, and the profile of a female head with fine blond hair was there in front of me, speaking across to the man with spectacles:

"Would you mind changing seats with me? Please?"

Not wanting to make a scene, there was nothing for me to do but scramble out of the way to permit the transfer. The man got out, the female got in and settled herself, and I sat down again just as the plane tilted for a bank.

She patted my arm and said, "Escamillo darling. Don't kiss me here. Good heavens, you're handsome in uniform."

"I haven't," I said coolly, "any intention of kissing you anywhere."

Her blue eyes were not quite wide open and a corner

of her mouth was turned up a little. Viewed objectively, there was nothing at all wrong with the scenery, but I was in no frame of mind to view Lily Rowan objectively. I have told elsewhere how I met her just outside the fence of an upstate pasture. The episode started with me in the pasture along with a bull, and the situation was such that when I reached the fence considerations of form and dignity were minor matters. Anyhow, I got over, rolled maybe ten yards and scrambled to my feet, and a girl in a yellow shirt and slacks clapped her hands sarcastically and drawled at me. "Beautiful, Escamillo! Do it again!"

That was Lily. One thing had led to another. Several others. Until finally . . .

But now—

She squeezed my arm and said, "Escamillo darling."

I gazed straight at her and said, "Lookit. The only reason I don't get up and ask one of our fellow passengers to change seats with me is that I am in uniform and the service has notions about dignity in public places, and I know quite well that you are capable of acting like a lunatic. I am going to read the paper."

I unfolded the *Times*. She was laughing in her throat, which I had once thought was an attractive sound, and she arranged herself in her seat so that her arm was against mine.

"Sometimes," she said, "I wish that bull had got you that day three years ago. I never dreamed, when I saw you tumbling over that fence, that it would ever come to this. You haven't answered my letters or telegrams. So I came to Washington to find out where you were, intending to go there—and here I am. Me, Lily Rowan! Escamillo, look at me!"

"I'm reading the paper."

"Good heavens, you're wonderful in uniform. Very

rugged. Doesn't it impress you that I found out you were taking this plane and got on before you did? Am I a smart girl or not?"

I didn't say anything.

"Answer me," she said with an edge to her voice.

She was capable of anything. "Yeah," I said, "you're smart."

"Thank you. I'm also smart enough to know that your being mad at me because I said that Ireland shouldn't give up any naval or air bases is phony. My father came here from Ireland and made eight million dollars building sewers—and I'm Irish and you know it, so your going sour on me on account of that is the bunk. I think you think you're tired of me. I have palled on you. Well?"

I kept my eyes on the paper. "I'm in the Army now, pet."

"So you are. Haven't I sent you forty telegrams offering to go and be near you and read aloud to you? Thinking you might be sick or something, haven't I been three times to see Nero Wolfe to find out if he was hearing from you? Which reminds me, what the dickens is the matter with him? He refuses to see me. And he likes me."

"He does not like you. He likes no woman."

"Well, he likes my being interested in his orchids. And besides, I wrote him that I had a case for him and would pay him myself. He wouldn't even talk to me on the phone."

I looked at her. "What kind of a case?"

A corner of her mouth went up. "Like to know?"

"Go to the devil."

"Now, Escamillo. Am I your bauble?"

"No."

"I am too. I like the way your nose twitches when

you smell a case. This is about a friend of mine, or anyway a girl I know, named Ann Amory. I was worried about her."

"I can't see you being worried about a girl named Ann Amory, or any girl except one named Lily Rowan."

Lily patted my arm. "That sounds more like you. Anyway, I wanted an excuse to see Nero Wolfe, and Ann was in trouble. All she really wanted was advice. She had found out something about somebody and wanted to know what to do about it."

"What had she found out about who?"

"I don't know. She wouldn't tell me. Her father used to work for my father, and I helped her out when he died. She works at the National Bird League and gets thirty dollars a week." Lily shivered. "Good lord, think of it, thirty dollars a week! Of course that's no worse than thirty dollars a day; you couldn't possibly live anyhow. She came and asked me to send her to a lawyer and she certainly was upset. All she would tell me was that she had learned something terrible about someone, but from several things she let slip I think it's her fiancé. I thought Nero Wolfe would be better for her than any lawyer."

"And he wouldn't see you?"

"No."

"Ann didn't mention any names at all?"

"No."

"Where does she live?"

"Downtown, not far from you—316 Barnum Street."

"Who is her fiancé?"

"Oh, I don't know." Lily patted my arm. "Listen, you big rugged hero. Where shall we have dinner tonight? My place?"

I shook my head. "I'm on duty. Your attitude on

bases in Ireland is subversive. For all I know, you're an Irish spy. I regard you as irresistible, but I've got my honor to think of. I warned you that day in the Methodist tent that my spiritual side—"

She cut me off and so it went. So it went for another hour, until we touched ground again at LaGuardia Airport. I wasn't able to duck her there. For the sake of decorum I split a taxi with her to Manhattan, but in front of the Ritz, where she had her own tower, and where I knew she would be disinclined to tear up sidewalks. I got myself transferred to another taxi with my bags and gave the driver the address of Wolfe's house on 35th Street.

In spite of the encounter with Lily, as I rolled downtown and then turned west, I'm here to tell you it was okay with me. I don't know why it seemed as if I'd been away a lot longer than two months, but it did. I recognized stores and buildings, as if I owned them, that I didn't remember ever bothering to look at before. I hadn't sent a wire because I thought it would be fun to surprise them, and naturally I was looking forward to seeing Theodore up in the plant rooms with the orchids, and Fritz in the kitchen stirring things in bowls and sniffing and tasting, and Nero Wolfe himself seated at his desk, frowning at a page of the atlas or maybe growling at a book he was reading— No, he wouldn't be in the office. He didn't come down from the plant rooms until six o'clock, so he would be up there with Theodore. I would say hello to Fritz in the kitchen and then sneak up to my room and wait until after I heard the elevator descending, bringing Wolfe down to the office.

Chapter 3

That was the worst shock I ever got in my life, bar none.

I let myself in with my key, which was still on my ring, dropped my bags in the hall, entered the office, and didn't believe my eyes. Stacks of unopened mail were on Wolfe's desk. I walked over to it and saw that it hadn't been dusted for ten years, and neither had mine. I turned around to face the door and felt myself swallowing. Either Wolfe or Fritz was dead, the only question was which. Next thing I knew I was in the kitchen, and what I saw there convinced me that they both were dead. They must be. The rows of pots and pans were dusty too, and the spice jars.

I swallowed again. I opened a cupboard door and saw not a damn thing but a dish of oranges and six cartons of prunes. I opened the refrigerator, and that finished it. There was nothing there but four heads of lettuce, four tomatoes, and a dish of applesauce. I dashed out and made for the stairs.

One flight up, both Wolfe's room and the spare were uninhabited, but the furniture looked normal. Same for the two rooms on the floor above, one of which was mine. I kept going, on up to the plant rooms. In the four growing-rooms there was nothing under the glass but orchids, hundreds of them in bloom, but in the potting-room I finally found a sign of human life, namely a man. It was Theodore Horstmann, on a stool at the bench, making entries in a propagation record book which I had formerly kept.

I demanded, "Where's Wolfe? Where's Fritz? What the hell's going on here?"

Theodore finished a word, blotted it, turned on the stool, and squeaked at me:

"Why, hello, Archie. They're out exercising. Only they call it training. They're out training."

"Are they well? Alive?"

"Of course they're alive. They're training."

"Training what?"

"Training each other. Or perhaps more accurately, training themselves. They're going into the Army, to fight. I am going to stay here as caretaker. Mr. Wolfe was going to dispose of the plants, but I persuaded him to leave them with me. Mr. Wolfe doesn't work with the plants any more; he only comes up here to sweat. He has to sweat all he can in order to reduce his weight, and then he has to get hardened up, so he and Fritz go over by the river and walk fast. Next week they're going to start to run. He is dieting and he has stopped drinking beer. Last week he caught cold but he's over it now. He won't buy any bread or cream or butter or sugar or lots of things and I have to buy my own meat."

"Where do they train?"

"Over by the river. Mr. Wolfe obtained permission from the authorities to train on a pier because the boys on the street ridiculed him. From seven to nine in the morning and four to six in the afternoon. Mr. Wolfe is very persistent. He spends the rest of the time up here sweating. He doesn't talk much, but I heard him telling Fritz that if two million Americans will kill ten Germans apiece—"

I had had enough of Theodore's squeak. I left him, went back down to the office, got a cloth and dusted my desk and chair, sat down and elevated my dogs, and scowled at the stacks of mail on Wolfe's desk.

Good God, I thought, what a homecoming this turned out to be. I might have known something like this would happen if I left him to manage himself. It is not only bad, it may be hopeless. The fathead. The big fat goop. And I told that general I know how to handle him. Now what am I going to do?

At 5:50 I heard the front door open and close, and footsteps in the hall, and there was Nero Wolfe looking in at me from the threshold with Fritz back of him.

"What are you doing here?" he boomed.

I'll never forget that sight as long as I live. I was speechless. He didn't exactly look smaller, he merely looked deflated. The pants were his own, an old pair of blue serge. The shoes were strangers, rough army style. The sweater was mine, a heavy maroon number that I had bought once for a camping trip, and in spite of his reduction of circumference it was stretched so tight that his yellow shirt showed through the holes.

I found my tongue to say, "Come in! Come on in!"

"I've given up the office for the time being," he said, and he and Fritz both turned and headed for the kitchen.

I sat there awhile, screwing up my lips and scowling, hearing noises they were making, and finally got up and moseyed out to join them. Apparently Wolfe had given up the dining-room too, for he and Fritz were both seated at the little table by the window eating prunes, with a bowl of lettuce and tomatoes, no dressing in sight, waiting for them. I propped myself against the long table, looking down at them, and managed a grin.

"Trying an experiment?" I asked pleasantly.

With his spoon Wolfe conveyed a prune seed from his mouth to the dish. He was looking at me and pretending not to. "How long," he demanded, "have you been a major?"

"Three days." I couldn't help staring at him. It was unbelievable. "They promoted me on account of my table manners. Theodore tells me you are going to join the Army. May I ask in what capacity?"

Wolfe had another prune in his mouth. When he got rid of the seed he said, "Soldier."

"You mean forward march and bang? Parachute troops? Commandos? Driving a jeep maybe—"

"That will do, Archie." His tone was sharp and his glance was too. He put down his spoon. "I am going to kill some Germans. I didn't kill enough in 1918. Whatever your reason for coming here—I presume it is your furlough before going overseas—I am sorry you came. I am quite aware of the physical difficulties that confront me, and I will tolerate no remarks from you. I am more keenly aware of them than you are. I am sorry you came, because I am undertaking a complicated adjustment in my habits, and your presence will make it more burdensome. I congratulate you on your promotion. If you are staying for dinner—"

"No, thank you," I said politely. "I've got a date for dinner. But I'll sleep here in my bed if you don't mind. I'll try not to annoy you—"

"Fritz and I go to bed at nine sharp."

"Okay. I'll take my shoes off downstairs. Much obliged for the fatted calf. I apologize for dusting off my desk and chair, but I was afraid I'd get my uniform dirty. My furlough is two weeks."

"I hope, Archie, you will understand—"

I didn't wait to hear it. If I had stayed there a second longer I would simply have had to cut loose.

Chapter 4

At Sam's Place, at the corner, I went first to the
phone booth and called Colonel Ryder at Governor's Island to tell him I was on the job, and then
settled myself at a table with a plate of beef stew and
two glasses of milk.

As I ate the stew I considered the situation. It was
not only tough, it was probably impossible. What had
happened was quite plain: Wolfe had simply put his
brains away in a drawer for the duration. He wasn't
going to do any thinking, because that was just work,
whereas dieting and going outdoors every day and
walking fast, getting ready to shoot some Germans—
that was heroic. And he had already gone so far with
it, and he was so damn bullheaded, that it looked hopeless. After mulling it over, I would have crossed it off
and got my bags and headed for Governor's Island, but
for two things: first, I had told the general I knew how
to handle him; and second, it looked as if he was going to
kill himself if I didn't stop him. If even one cell of his
brain had been working—but it wasn't.

I thought of appealing for help, to Marko Vukcic or
Raymond Plehn or Lewis Hewitt, or even Inspector
Cramer, but of course that was no good. Any kind of

appeal or argument would only make him stubborner, since he was refusing to think. The only thing that would turn the trick was to manage somehow to get his brain going. I knew from experience what a job that was, and he had never been in a condition to compare with the one he was in now. Futhermore I was handicapped by having been away for two months and not knowing who had called at the office or tried to, or whether there had been any current events.

That, I thought, was one possibility, so after I had paid my check I went to the phone booth and called Inspector Cramer. He said he thought I was in the Army, and I said I thought so too, and then I asked him: "You got any good crimes on hand? Murders or robberies or even missing persons?"

That didn't get me anywhere. Either he had nothing promising or he wasn't telling me. I went out to the sidewalk and stood there scowling at a taxi driver. It was cold, darned cold for the middle of March, and flurries of snow were scooting around, and I had no overcoat. As a forlorn hope, because there was nothing else to do, I climbed in the taxi and told the driver to take me to 316 Barnum Street. It wasn't actually a hope at all, just a stab in the dark because there wasn't any light.

There was nothing about the outside of the building to warn me of the goofy assortment of specimens inside, merely an ordinary-looking old brick structure of four stories, the kind that had once been a private house but somewhere around the time I was born had been made into flats, with the vestibule fitted up with mailboxes and bell buttons. The card in one of the slots said *Pearl O. Chack* and beneath it in smaller letters, *Amory*. I pushed the button, shoved the door open when the click sounded, and was proceeding along the hall when a door toward the rear was suddenly flung open and somebody's female ancestor appeared on the threshold. If you had deducted for skin and bones there wouldn't have been more than 20 pounds left of her for tissue and internal parts all together. Straggling ends of white hair made a latticework for her piercing black eyes to see through, and there was no question about her being able to see. As I headed for her she snapped at me before I got there.

"What do you want?"

I produced a smile. "I would like to see—"

She chopped me off. "She sent you! I know she did! I thought it was her. She plays that trick sometimes. Goes out and rings the bell, thinking I won't suspect it's her. She wants to tell me she thinks I killed her mother. I know what she wants! If she ever says that to me once, just once, I'll have her arrested! You tell her that! Go up and tell her that now!"

She was drawing back and shutting the door. I got a foot on the sill. "Just a minute, lady. I'll go up and tell her anything you want me to. You mean Miss Amory? Ann Amory?"

"Ann? My granddaughter?" The black eyes darted at me through the white latticework. "Certainly not! You're not fooling me—"

"I know I'm not, Mrs. Chack, but you've got me wrong. I want to see your granddaughter, that's all. I came to see Ann. Is she—"

"I don't believe it!" she snapped, and banged the door shut. I could have stopped it with my foot, but it seemed doubtful if that was the proper course under the circumstances, and besides, I had heard noises upstairs. Immediately after the door banged there were footsteps coming down, and by the time I had moved to the foot of the stairs a young man was there at my level.

Evidently he had intended to say something, but at sight of the uniform changed to something else.

"Oh," he said in surprise, "the Army? I expected—"

He stopped, looking at me. As to clothes he was careless and maybe not even too clean in a bright light, but otherwise you might have expected to find his picture as a back on a football team. Except he was a little light for it.

"Not at present on duty," I said. "Why, what did you expect, the Navy?"

He laughed. "I just meant I didn't expect to see an Army officer. Not here. And I heard you asking to see Miss Amory, and I didn't know she knew any Army officers."

"Do you know Miss Amory?"

"Sure I know her. I live here. Two flights up." He extended a hand. "My name's Leon Furey."

"Mine's Archie Goodwin." We shook hands. "Do you happen to know if Miss Amory is at home?"

"She's up on the roof." He was taking me in. "Not the Archie Goodwin that works for Nero Wolfe?"

"That used to. Before I changed clothes. What is Miss Amory doing—"

A voice cut in from up above:

"Who is it, Leon? Bring him up!"

It was a borderline husky voice, the kind that requires further evidence before deciding the question, man or woman. The young man's head pivoted for a quick look up the stairs and then turned back to me, and his face broke into a grin. It seemed likely that he regarded it as an engaging grin, or maybe even charming. The vote for him in the Larchmont Women's Club would have stood about 92 to 11. He came closer to me and lowered his voice.

"I suppose you know you're in a bughouse? My

advice is to beat it. I'll take a message for Miss Amory—"

"Leon!" the voice came down. "Bring him up here!"

"I'd like to see Miss Amory now," I said, and started to by-pass Leon, but he shrugged his shoulders with masculine charm and started back upstairs, with me following. In the hall one flight up, standing in an open door, was the owner of the voice. The clothes, a brown woolen dress that might have been worn at the inauguration of McKinley, apparently settled the man or woman question, but aside from that she was built to play end or tackle on the same team with Leon. Also she stood more like a soldier than I did or was likely to.

"What's this?" she demanded as we approached. "I don't know you. Come in here."

Leon called her "Miss Leeds," and informed her that I was Archie Goodwin, formerly Nero Wolfe's assistant, now Major Goodwin of the United States Army, but there was no knowing whether she got it, because she had her back turned, marching inside the apartment, taking it for granted we would follow, which we did. The furniture of the big room she led us into must have dated from McKinley's childhood, and there was plenty of it. I sat down because she told me to as if she meant it, taking in the museum with a glance. To finish it off, there was a marble-topped table in the center of the room, with nothing on it but a dead hawk with its wings stretched out. Not a stuffed hawk, just a dead one, just lying there. I guess I stared at it, because she said, "He kills them for me."

I asked politely, "Are you a taxidermist, Miss Leeds?"

"Oh, no, she likes pigeons," Leon said in an informative tone. He was sitting on a piano stool with a plush top. "There are seventy thousand pigeons in Manhattan, and about ninety hawks, and they kill the pigeons. The hawks keep coming. They live on the ledges of buildings, and I kill them for Miss Leeds. I got that one—"

"That's none of your business," Miss Leeds told me brusquely. "I heard you talking to Mrs. Chack and asking for Ann Amory. I want you to understand that I do not wish any investigation into the death of my mother. It is not necessary. Mrs. Chack is crazy. Both crazy and malicious. She tells people that I think she killed my mother, but I don't. I don't think anyone killed my mother. She died of old age. I have explained thoroughly that no investigation is necessary, and I want it understood—"

"He's not a policeman," Leon put in. "He's an Army officer, Miss Leeds."

"What's the difference?" she demanded. "Army or police, it's all the same." She was regarding me sternly. "Do you understand me, young man? You tell the mayor I want this stopped. I own this house and I own nine houses on this block and I pay my taxes, and I don't intend to be annoyed. My mother wrote the mayor and she wrote the papers a thousand times what they ought to do. They ought to keep the hawks out of the city. I want to ask you what is being done about that. Well?"

I should have smiled at her, but she just wasn't anything to smile at. So I looked her in the eye and said, "Miss Leeds, you want facts. Okay, here's three facts. One. This is the first I ever heard of hawks. Two. This is the first I ever heard of your mother. Three. I came here to see Ann Amory, and Leon tells me she's up on the roof." I stood up. "If I see any hawks up there, I'll catch 'em alive and wring their necks. And I'll tell the mayor what you said."

I walked out to the hall and along that to the next flight of stairs.

Chapter 5

The hall above and the one above that were each lit by a single unshaded bulb in a wall socket, but when I opened the door at the stairs to the roof, and passed through and closed it behind me, I was in darkness. I felt my way up with my feet on the wooden treads, found a latch at the top and opened a door, and was on the roof. Blinking at flakes of snow the wind was tossing around, and seeing nothing anywhere that might have been called Ann Amory, I headed for what looked like a penthouse to my left. Light was showing at the edges of a shaded window, and when I got to the door I could make out a sign painted on it:

> RACING PIGEON LOFT
> ROY DOUGLAS
> KEEP OUT!

Since it said keep out, naturally my impulse was to go on in, but I restrained it and knocked. A man's voice came asking who it was, and I called that it was company for Miss Amory, and the door swung open.

That house seemed to be inhabited exclusively by conclusion-jumpers. Without giving me a chance to in-

troduce myself the young man who had opened the
door, and closed it again after I entered, began telling
me that he couldn't possibly spare any more for at least
four months, that he was willing and eager to do anything he could to help win the war but he had already
sent me 40 birds and had to keep his stock for breeding,
and he didn't see why the Army didn't understand.

Meanwhile I was surveying. Boxes and bags were
stacked around, and shelves were cluttered with various kinds of items that I had never seen before. A door
in the far wall had a sign on it: *Do Not Open*. A wire
cage, more like a coop, with a pigeon in it, was on a table,
and on a chair by the table was a girl. She was looking
up at me with wide-open brown eyes. As for the young
man, he wasn't in Leon Furey's class as a physical
specimen, and they had short-changed him a little on
his chin, but he would pass. I stopped him in the middle
of his speech.

"You're wasting it, brother. I'm not a pigeon collec-
tor. My name is Archie Goodwin and I came to see Miss
Amory." I put out a hand. "You're Roy Douglas?" We
shook. "Nice chilly place you've got here. Miss Amory?"

"I don't know you," the girl said in the kind of voice
I like, "do I?"

"You do now," I assured her. "Anyhow, you don't
need to, because I'm only a messenger boy. Lily Rowan
wants you to come and have dinner with her, and sent
me to get you."

"Lily Rowan?" The brown eyes looked puzzled.
"But why—she sent you for me?"

"Right." I made it casual. "Since you know Lily, you
may be surprised she didn't send a brigadier general,
but there was nothing around but majors."

Ann laughed, and it was the kind of laugh I like.
Then she looked at the pigeon in the coop, and at

Roy, and back at me. "I don't know," she said uncertainly. "I've already had dinner. You mean she wants to see me?" She got up. "I suppose I'd better—" She made up her mind. "But I can go—You don't need to bother—"

I got her out of there. Evidently Roy did not regard the proceeding with enthusiasm, and neither did the pigeon, but she came, after a little more discussion. Roy lighted us down to the top floor with a flashlight and then returned to his loft. On the ground floor I waited in the hall while Ann went in to speak to her grandmother and get a coat, and when she required less than five minutes for it I liked that too. On the street she didn't take my arm and she didn't try to keep step. So far she was batting a thousand. We got a taxi at the corner.

The next test was a little stiffer. As we turned uptown on Fifth Avenue I said, "Now it can be told. Here was the situation. I wanted a private talk with you. I couldn't talk with you in the presence of Roy and the pigeon. I knew we couldn't have a talk in your apartment because I had met your grandmother. If I had asked you to go somewhere with me, you would have refused. So I invented an invitation from Lily Rowan. Now what are we going to do?"

Her eyes were wide open at me. "Do you mean— But how did you know—"

"Just a minute. The question was rhetorical. I suppose you've heard of Nero Wolfe, the detective. I worked for him up to two months ago, when I joined the Army. Today Lily Rowan told me that you asked her to send you to a lawyer, and she has been trying to arrange for you to see Nero Wolfe, but Mr. Wolfe has been occupied. I think I can fix it. He is a very busy man, if you'll just tell me what it's about—"

"Oh," she said. She gazed at me. Finally she shook her head. "I don't—I couldn't tell you."

"Why not? You're in trouble, aren't you?"

"Yes. I am."

"Didn't you intend to tell the lawyer you asked Lily to send you to?"

"Yes."

"Well, Nero Wolfe is worth ten lawyers. Any ten."

"But you're not Nero Wolfe. You're just a handsome young man in a uniform." She shook her head again. "Really I couldn't."

"You're wrong, sister. I'm handsome, but I'm not just handsome. However, we've got all night. Say we try this. We've both had dinner. Say we go somewhere and dance. Between dances I'll explain to you how bright I am, and try to win your confidence, and get you to drink as much as possible to loosen your tongue. That might get us somewhere."

She laughed. "Where would we go to dance?"

"Anywhere. The Flamingo Club."

I told the driver.

She turned out to be a pretty fair dancer, but not much at bending the elbow. The dinner mob already had the place nearly filled, but I declared a priority on a table in a corner that was being held for some deb's delight, and when he turned up with his Abigail Spriggs alumna I just stared him out of it into the jungle. Ann and I got along fine. Socially the evening was absolutely okay, but fundamentally I was there on business and from that angle it was close to a washout.

Not that I didn't gather information. I learned that the pigeon I had seen in the coop was a Sion-Stassart pigeon named Dusky Diana, the holder of nine diplomas and the mother of four 500-mile winners, and Roy Douglas had paid $90 for her, and she had hit a chimney three days ago in a gust of wind while out exercising, and was being nursed. Also that there had been a feud between Miss Leed's mother and Mrs. Chack, Ann's grandmother, dating from the 19th century, which Mrs. Chack and Miss Leeds were carrying on. The cause of the feud was that Chack fed squirrels and Leeds fed pigeons, both using Washington Square as a base of operations. They were both there every morning soon after dawn, staying a couple of hours, and again in the late afternoon. Mrs. Chack could stay later than Mrs. Leeds, often until after dark, because pigeons went to bed earlier than squirrels, and it was Mrs. Chack's daily triumph when the enemy had to give up and go home. The bitterest and deepest aspect of the feud was that Mrs. Chack had accused Miss Leed's mother of poisoning squirrels on December 9, 1905, and tried to have her arrested. That date had not been forgotten and never would be.

Also I learned that Miss Leed's mother had died on December 9, three months ago. Mrs. Chack had announced to the neighborhood that it had been a visitation of God's slow anger at an ancient crime, and whisperings that got to the ears of the police had resulted in a discreet investigation, but nothing had come of it. Here I thought I had something up a tree, in fact I was sure I had, from the way Ann acted, but that was as far as I got. Nor was she discussing her fiancé, even to the extent of admitting she had one. Evidently she was sticking to it that I was just handsome.

All of a sudden, around midnight, I realized something. What brought it to my attention was the fact that I was noticing the smell of her hair while we were dancing. I was even sniffing it. It had startled me so I bumped into a couple on the right and nearly toppled them over. There I was—presumably on duty, working, and sore at her for being too damn stubborn to open up—and there I was deliberately smelling hair! That was a hell of a note. I steered her around to an edge, off the floor and back to the table, and sat her down and called for the check.

"Oh," she said, "must we go?"

"Look here," I told her, looking in her wide-open eyes, "you're giving me a run-around. Maybe you did the same to Lily Rowan, or she did to me. Are you in trouble, or aren't you?"

"Why, yes. Yes, Archie, I am."

"What kind of trouble? A run in your stocking?"

"No, really. It's—real trouble. Honestly."

"But you're not telling me about it?"

She shook her head. "I can't. Honestly I can't. I mean—I don't want to. You see, you *are* young and handsome. It's something terrible—I don't mean it's terrible about me—it's something terrible about someone."

"Is it about the death of Miss Leed's mother?"

"It—" She stopped. Then she went on. "Yes, it is. But that's all I'll tell you. If you're going to be like this—"

The waiter brought the change, and I took my share. Then I said, "Okay. The reason I'm like this, I caught myself smelling your hair. Not only that, for the last half-hour I've had a different attitude toward our dancing. You may have noticed it."

"Yes, I—did."

"Very well. I didn't. Until just now. I admit it's possible there is romance ahead of us. Or you may break my heart and ruin my life. Anything can happen. But not yet. What I want to know now is, what time do you quit work?"

She was smiling at me. "I leave the office at five o'clock."

"And what, go home?"

She nodded. "I usually get home a little before five-thirty. And take a bath, and start cooking dinner. This time of year, grandmother gets home from the Square around seven, and I have dinner ready for her. Sometimes Roy or Leon eats with us."

"Could you eat early tomorrow and come to Nero Wolfe's house at seven o'clock? And tell him about the trouble you're in? Tell him all about it?"

She frowned at me, hesitating. I covered her hand, on the tablecloth, with mine. "Look, sister," I said, "it's possible that you're headed for something terrible yourself. I'm not trying to pretend—"

I stopped because I felt a presence, and I felt eyes. I glanced up, and there were the eyes looking down at me, one on each side of Lily Rowan's pretty little nose.

I tried to grin at her. "Why—hello there—"

"You," Lily said, in a tone to cut my throat. "On duty, huh? You louse!"

I think she was going to smack me. Anyhow, it was obvious that she wasn't going to care what she did, and intended to proceed without delay, so it was merely a question of who moved first and fastest. I was out of my chair, on my feet across the table from her, in half a second flat, with a gesture to Ann, and Ann passed that test too, a fairly tough one, with flying colors. As fast as I moved she was with me, and before even Lily Rowan could get any commotion started we had my cap from the hat-check girl and were out on the sidewalk.

As the taxi rolled away with us I patted Ann's hand and said, "Good girl. Apparently she was upset about something."

"She was jealous," Ann chuckled. "My lord, she was jealous. Lily Rowan jealous of me!"

When I left her at 316 Barnum Street, it was agreed that she would be at Nero Wolfe's place at 7:00 the next day. Even so, as the taxi took me back to 35th Street, I was not in a satisfactory frame of mind, and it wasn't improved by finding pinned to my pillowcase a note which said:

> *Dear Archie, Miss Rowan telephoned four times, and when I told her you were not here she said I was a liar. I am sorry there is no bacon or ham or pancake flour or anything like that in the house.*
>
> *Fritz*

Chapter 6

I slept because I always sleep, but my nerves must have been in bad shape, because when my eyes opened and read the clock at 6:50 I was immediately wide awake. I would have given my next two promotions for the satisfaction of planting myself in the downstairs hall and glaring at Wolfe and Fritz as they left on their way to the training field, but knowing that would be a bad blunder in strategy I restrained myself. All I did was open my door so I could hear noises, and when, promptly at 7:00 I heard the street door open and close, I went to a window and leaned out for a look. And there they went, off toward the river, Wolfe in the blue serge pants and my maroon sweater and heavy shoes, no hat, at a gait he probably thought was a stride, swinging his arms. It was simply too damn pathetic.

On that heavy gray March morning my Ann Amory operation looked pretty hopeless, but it was all I had, so I prepared to give it the works. After orange juice and ham and eggs and pancakes and two cups of coffee at Sam's Place, I went back to the house and spent an hour at the typewriter and telephone cleaning up a few personal matters that had collected in my absence, and was just finishing up when, a little after 9:00, here came the

Commandos back. My plan was to ignore them entirely, so I didn't turn around when footsteps in the hall stopped at the open office door, but Wolfe's voice sounded:

"Good morning, Archie. I spend the day upstairs. Did you sleep well?"

It was his regular morning question that he had asked me 4,000 times, and it made me homesick. I admit it. It softened me up. I swiveled my chair to face him, but that hardened me again, just one look at him.

"Fine, thanks," I said coldly. "You messed my drawers up, I suppose looking for that sweater. I have something to say to you. I am speaking for the United States Army. There is one thing you are better qualified to do than anyone else, in connection with undercover enemy activities in this country. It is a situation requiring brains, which you used to have and sometimes used. The Commander in Chief, the Secretary of War, and the General Staff, also Sergeant York, respectfully request you to cut the comedy and begin using them. You are wrong if you think your sudden appearance in the front lines will make the Germans laugh themselves to death. They have no sense of humor."

I thought that might make him mad enough to forget himself and enter the office, and if I once got him in there it would be a point gained, but he merely stood and scowled at me.

"You said," he growled, "that you're on furlough."

"I did not. You ought to be ashamed of yourself. That shows the condition you're in. A thousand times, right in this room, I've heard you give people hell for inexact statements. What I said was that my furlough is two weeks. I did not say that I'm on it now. Nor did I mention—"

"Pfui!" he sputtered scornfully, and turned and

started up the stairs. Which was another phenomenon I had never seen before, him mounting those stairs. It had cost him $7,000 to install the elevator.

I got my cap and left the house and started to work.

I tried to inject some enthusiasm into the day's operations, and I did do my best, but at no point did any probability appear that I was going to turn up anything that could be used for a lever to pry Wolfe loose. It was a different problem from any that had ever confronted me before, because, since he was hell-bent for heroism, no appeal to his cupidity would work. In the condition he had got himself into, the only weak spot where I might break through was his vanity.

I learned from friends at Centre Street that the investigation of Mrs. Leeds's death had never gone beyond the precinct, so I went there and made inquiries. The sergeant didn't bother to look up the record. Nothing to it. The doctor had certified coronary thrombosis at the age of 87, and the neighborhood gossip about Mrs. Chack pinch-hitting for the vengeance of God because she got impatient with Him for waiting so long was the bunk.

Around noon I dropped in at 316 Barnum Street, and found Leon Furey still in bed, or anyhow still in pajamas. He said he had to sleep late because he did his hawk hunting mostly at night. I learned that killing hawks was his only visible means of support, that the Army had turned him down on account of a leaky valve, that Roy Douglas lived on the floor above him, the one next to the roof, and a few other items, but nothing that seemed likely to help me any. I found Roy up on the roof, in his loft. He wouldn't let me in and wasn't inclined for conversation. He said he was busy working on the widower system, and all I got out of him was that the widower system was a method of keeping a male

pigeon away from his mate for a certain period, and
letting him in with her for a couple of minutes just
before shipping him to the liberation point for a race,
the result being that he flew to get back as he had never
flown before. I disapproved of it on moral grounds, but
that didn't seem to interest Roy either, so I left him to
his widower system, descended again to the street, and
began exploring the community.

For over three hours I collected neighborhood gossip, and it wasn't worth a dime a bushel. I didn't even
get any significant dirt, let alone useful information. On
the question of the death of old Mrs. Leeds, fourteen of
them divided as follows:

> 4 Mrs. Chack killed her.
> 1 Miss Leeds killed her.
> 6 She died of old age.
> 3 She died of meanness.

No majority for anybody or anything. No nothing. I
went home, arriving a little before 5:00, to think it over
and decide whether it was worth while springing Ann
on Wolfe at all and as I stood in the office frowning at
the dust on Wolfe's desk, the doorbell rang. I went and
pulled the curtain aside for a look through the glass
panel, and there was Roy Douglas on the stoop. My
heart skipped a beat. Was something going to break? I
pulled the door open and invited him in.

He acted embarrassed, as if he had something he
wanted to say but wasn't quite sure what it was. I took
him to the office and dusted off a chair for him, and he
sat down and opened his mouth for air a couple of times
and then said:

"I guess I wasn't very courteous down there at the
loft today. I never am very polite when I'm working

with the birds. You see, it makes them nervous to have strangers around."

I nodded sympathetically. "Me too. By the way, I forgot to ask, how's Dusky Diana coming along?"

"Oh, she's much better. She'll be all right." He squinted at me. "I suppose Miss Amory told you about her?"

"Yeah, she told me a lot of interesting things."

He shifted in his chair. Then he cleared his throat. "You were with her all evening, weren't you?"

"Sure, I stuck around."

"I saw you when you came back. When you brought her home. From my window."

"Did you? It was pretty late."

"I know it was. But I—You see, I was worried about her. I am worried about her. I think she's in some kind of trouble or something, and I wondered if that was why she went to see that Lily Rowan."

"You might ask her."

He shook his head. "She won't tell me. But I'm sure she's in some kind of trouble, the way she acts. I don't know Miss Rowan, so I can't go and ask her, but I know you, that is I've met you, and if you were with them last evening—and then your coming to see me today—I thought you might tell me. You see, I've got a right to know about it, a kind of a right, because we're engaged to be married."

My brows went up. "You are? You and Miss Amory?"

"Yes."

"Congratulations."

"Thank you." He squinted at me. "So I wondered why you came to see me, and I thought maybe it was to tell me something about her, or ask me something, and that made me wonder—Anyhow, if you know whether she's in trouble I wish you'd tell me."

Except for the fact that I had solved the mystery of Ann's fiancé, or rather it had solved itself, that certainly didn't sound as if Roy's visit was going to break anything. However, since I had him there, I thought I might as well see what he had concealed on his person, so I proceeded to treat him as a friend. I told him I was sorry I couldn't help him out any on the nature of Ann's difficulty, if any, and casually guided the conversation in the direction of the inhabitants of 316 Barnum Street. That proved to be a boomerang. The minute we arrived at that address he got started on pigeons, and then did he talk!

I learned things. He had been in the fancy, as he put it, since boyhood. Mrs. Leeds had built the loft for him and kept him going, and now Miss Leeds was carrying on. His birds had won a total of 116 diplomas in young bird races and 63 diplomas in old bird races. One year his Village Susie, a Blue Check Grooter, had returned first in the Dayton Great National, with 3,864 birds, 512 lofts competing. He had lost fourteen birds in the big smash in the Trenton 300-mile special last year. The best racing pigeons in the world, in his opinion, were the Dickinson strain of Sion-Stassarts—Dusky Diana was one.

I couldn't get him off it. As the clock on the wall crept along toward 6:00 I began to think I'd have to pick him up and carry him outdoors, since Wolfe would come in from training soon after 6:00 and I didn't want him there. But that problem was solved for me. At 5:55 the doorbell rang, and Roy got up and said he would be going, and followed me out to the front. I pulled the curtain aside for a look, and what did I see on the stoop but Lily Rowan, and she had seen me.

I slipped the chain in the socket so the door would only open four inches, let it come that far, and announced through the crack:

"Air raid alarm. Go home and get under the bed. I'm on—"

Her hand came in through the crack, her arm nearly up to the elbow.

"Shut it on that," she said savagely. "Let me in."

"No, girlie, I—"

"Let me in! Do you want me to yell it for the whole neighborhood—"

"Yell what?"

"There's been a murder!"

"You mean there will be a murder. Some day—"

"Archie! You damned idiot! I tell you Ann Amory has been murdered! If you don't—"

There was a noise from Roy at my elbow. I pushed him aside, slipped the chain off, let Lily through, shut the door, and got her by the shoulders, gripping her good.

"Spill it," I told her. "If you think you're putting on a charade—"

"Quit hurting me!" she spat. Then she was quiet. "All right, keep on hurting me. Go on. Harder."

"Spill it, my love."

"I am spilling it. I went there to see Ann. When I rang the bell the latch didn't click, so I rang another bell and got in. The door of her apartment was standing a little open, so I knocked once and then went in. I thought she must be there because I had phoned her office and she said she would get home before five-thirty, and it was a quarter to six. She was there all right. She was there on the floor propped up against a chair with a scarf tied around her throat and her tongue hanging out and her eyes popping. She was dead. I saw she was dead and I—"

Roy Douglas went. He did it so quick, pulled the door open and scooted, that I didn't even get a chance to make a grab for him.

"Goddamn it," I said. I turned Lily loose and glanced at my wrist—6:02. If I beat it with her it would be just my luck for Wolfe to be approaching and see me. Lily was sputtering:

"I tell you, Archie, it was the most awful—"

"Shut up." I opened the door to the front room, steered her inside, and closed the door. "You do what I tell you, girlie, or I swear to God I'll scalp you. Sit down and don't breathe. Nero Wolfe will be coming in and I don't want him to know you're here. No, sit there, away from the window. I want to know one thing. Did you kill her?"

"No."

"Look at me. You didn't?"

"No."

"Okay."

"Archie—"

"Shut up."

I sat on the edge of a chair and put my fists on my knees and stared at the wall. I can't think with my eyes closed the way Wolfe does. In maybe three minutes I thought I had it, at least a sketch of it, if only it hadn't been for that damn Douglas kid. It all depended on him.

I looked at Lily. "Keep your voice low so we can hear the door open. You'd better whisper. How often have you been to the apartment?"

"Only once. A long time ago. I love you like this, Arch—"

"Save it for Christmas. Whose bell did you ring?"

"I don't know. One of the upper—"

"Did anybody see you going in or coming out?"

"I don't know about going in. I think not. I'm sure

they didn't coming out because I looked around and glanced up the stairs."

"Does anybody there know you? Besides Ann?"

"Mrs. Chack does, that's all. Ann's grandmother."

"Was anybody—hold it."

The street door was opening. It closed again, and I heard Wolfe's voice, and a murmur of Fritz's. Footsteps went down the hall and the door to the kitchen opened and closed.

I went noiselessly to the door to the hall and eased it open. The one to the kitchen was shut, and sounds came from beyond it. I beckoned to Lily and when she joined me whispered in her ear, "Fast *and* silent. Understand?" and tiptoed to the front door and got it open without a sound. Lily slipped through and me after her, I shut the door with only a faint click, and we went down the steps to the sidewalk and turned east. She had to trot to keep up. When we reached the avenue and turned the corner I got her into a doorway.

"Now. Was anyone standing around the entrance when you went in?"

"Standing around? No. But what—"

"Don't talk. I'm busy. You're noticeable. Did anyone notice you going in or coming out?"

"I don't think so. If they did I didn't notice them."

"Okay. I'm leaving you. Here's your program. Go some place out of town, not far, Long Island or Westchester. Leave a note for me at the Ritz telling me where, but don't tell anyone else. I—"

"You mean go now?"

"Right now. Pack a bag and go. Within an hour."

"You go to hell." She had my arm in both hands. "You darned nut, didn't I run to you in my hour of need? I'm going to have a drink, several drinks, and you're going to have some with me. What do you think I—"

I tried to bull it through, but nothing doing. She balked good, and time was precious. So I said, "Listen, angel. I've got a job to do and you've got to help. I haven't time to explain it. Do as I say, and I'll get a week-end leave Saturday and you can write your ticket, anything short of rowing on the lake in Central Park."

"This coming Saturday?"

"Yes."

"An absolutely unqualified promise?"

"Yes, damn it."

"Gentlemen prefer blondes. Kiss me good-by."

I made it a quick one, dashed across the sidewalk to a taxi, and told the driver corner of Barnum and Christopher, and step on it. My watch said 6:15. Roy had 13 minutes start on me.

Chapter 7

On account of Roy Douglas, there was a mighty slim hope of being able to fill in my sketch, but when I jumped from the cab at the corner and hotfooted it for Number 316 and saw there was no sign of anything unusual, the chances looked slightly better. The odds against me were still about 20 to 1. If anyone else, including Roy, had beat me to it and called the cops or a doctor or even the neighbors, or if grandma had come home early, or if 17 other things, my plan was a washout.

It would have been a swell break if the door had been unlatched, but it wasn't, so I pushed the *Chack-Amory* button, not daring to risk one of the others, and in about five seconds the click sounded. That might have been either good or bad, and there was no time to speculate. I entered and went down the hall, and there was Roy standing in the open door of the Chack apartment, his face pasty and twitching, trembling all over. Before he could say anything I shoved him inside and closed the door, touching it only with a knuckle. He looked as if he might start screaming. I steered him out of the little hall into a room and to a chair, and pushed him into it.

"She's dead," he said hoarsely. "I can't—look at her."

"Keep quiet," I commanded him. "Understand? Keep quiet. I know things about this you don't know."

I made a survey. There was no disorder, no sign of a scrap. I didn't blame Roy for not being able to look at Ann, because it wasn't actually Ann. It was only what was left, and it didn't resemble Ann at all. Lily had mentioned the two main aspects, the tongue and the eyes. The upper part of the body was sort of propped up against the front of an upholstered chair, and the blue woolen scarf around the throat had a knot under the left ear. Approaching and kneeling down, it took me ten seconds to make sure that it was a body and not a girl. It was still as warm as life.

I returned to Roy. He was slumped in the chair with his head hanging, and I doubted if there was enough stiffness in his spine to lift his head to look at me, so I lowered myself to one knee to look at him.

"Listen, Roy," I said, "we've got to do some things. How long ago did you get here?"

He stared at me. "I don't know," he muttered. "I don't know. I came straight here."

"How did you get in?"

"In where? Oh—my key—"

"No, in here. This apartment."

"The door was open."

"Wide open?"

"I don't know—no, not wide open. Just open a little."

"Did you see anybody? Did anybody see you?"

"No, I didn't see anybody."

"You didn't call anyone, phone anyone? A doctor? The police?"

"A doctor?" He squinted at me. "She's dead, isn't she?"

"Yeah, she's dead. You didn't call the police?"

He shook his head vaguely. "I didn't—I wasn't—"

"Okay. Hold it. Stay where you are." I got erect and glanced around, and through an open door saw a corner of a bed. I crossed over and into the bedroom, sat down on a stool at a dressing-table, got my notebook and pencil from my inside breast pocket, and wrote on a sheet of the book:

Dear Ann—

Sorry, I'll have to change the arrangement. Don't come to Nero Wolfe's place at seven. Instead, I'll come for you around 5:30.

Archie

I tore out the sheet and folded it and crinkled it a little, then leaned closer to the mirror to see better, separated a lock of my hair from the mop I wore, maybe eight or ten hairs, twisted them around my finger, and yanked them out. Returning to the living-room, I squatted in front of the body, shoved the folded paper down the front of the dress, next to the skin, and tucked the lock of hair behind the scarf around the throat, under the right jaw. The scarf was so tight it took force to do it. I patted her on the shoulder and murmured at her, "All right, Ann, we'll get the bastard. Or bitch, as the case may be." Then I straightened up and proceeded to make fingerprints. Three sets would be enough, I thought, one on the arm of a chair, one on the edge of the table, and one on the cover of a magazine on the table. My watch said 6:37. If Mrs. Chack happened to return early from squirrel-feeding, she might come any minute, and it would be a crime to spoil it now.

I went over to Roy. "How are you? Can you walk?"

"Walk?" He had quit trembling. "Where is there to walk to? We've got to get—"

"Look here," I said. "Ann's dead. Somebody killed her. We want to find out who did it. Don't we?"

"Yes." He showed his teeth. It was like a dog snarling in its sleep. "I do."

"Then come along." I took hold of his arm. "We're going somewhere."

"But we can't—just leave her—"

"We can't help her any. We'll notify the police, but not from here. I tell you I know something about this. Come on, let's get going."

I hefted his arm, and he got to his feet, and I headed him for the door. I had decided against fingerprints there, so I used my hankerchief for wiping the knob and turning it, and the same on the outside. The hall was deserted and there was no sound of life. I hustled Roy along, got him out to the street, and turned toward Christopher, taking a normal pedestrian gait. My heart was pumping. I admit it. It looked as if I was going to put it over, with only one item left, to dispose of Roy for 24 hours.

I took him into a bar on Seventh Avenue, got him onto a chair at a table, ordered two double Scotches, told him I'd be back in a minute, and went to the phone booth and dialed a number.

"Lily? Me. Are you packing?"

"Yes, damn you. What—"

"Me talking. No time for explanations. All for now is, don't leave till I phone you again. Okay?"

"Did you go—"

"Sorry. Busy. Stay there till I phone you."

Back at the table, Roy was fingering his glass and beginning to tremble again. I saw that he got the drink down, all of it, and then leaned forward to him:

"Now listen, Roy. Get this. You can trust me. You know who I am, and you know who Nero Wolfe is. That ought to be enough. We're going to find out who killed Ann, and you've got to help us. You want to, don't you?"

He was frowning. The kick of the drink was putting color in his face. "But the police—" he began.

"Sure, the police will be on it any minute, as soon as Mrs. Chack gets home. And I'll phone them myself, and I'll be working with them. But I've got a line on this that I don't dare tell them about. Do you know Lily Rowan? By sight?"

"No, I've never seen her."

"Well, I think she's going to skip. I'm sure of it. She lives at the Ritz. We'll go there now, and if she comes out with luggage I'll point her out to you, and you follow her. Hang onto her no matter where she goes. Will you do that?"

His cheeks were flushed. Apparently he was no soak. He said, "I've never followed anybody. I don't know how."

"All it takes is intelligence, and you've got that." I got out my wallet, extracted five twenties, and handed them to him. "I would do it myself, only I must do something else. And this is important, remember this: don't try to report to me until Thursday morning at nine o'clock, and then report by telephone, no matter where you are, and then either to Nero Wolfe or to me. Nobody else." I finished my drink. "You've got to do this, Roy. I'll make a phone call and then we'll go. Well? Have you got it in you?"

He nodded. "I'll do my best."

"Good for you. I'll be back in a minute."

I went to the phone booth and dialed the number again.

"Lily, my angel? Me. Get this. In twenty minutes,

maybe less, I'll be on the sidewalk at the Madison Avenue entrance of the Ritz, and Roy Douglas will be with me. He's the guy that was there when you arrived at Wolfe's house. I'll point you out to him and he'll follow you, tail you. I want him out of town for a day or so, and this is the only way I can work it. When you take a taxi to the railroad station—"

"I'm not going to a railroad station. I'm going to the Worthington at Greenwich, and I'm going to drive—"

"No. Take a train. This is part of the deal, or the deal's off. Be sure he doesn't loose you. When you buy your ticket at Grand Central, be sure he's close enough to hear where to, and be sure he makes the train. Take a day coach, no parlor car. He'll stay at the Worthington too. Keep an eye on him, but don't let him know you know he's tailing you. Don't do any horseback riding or anything to frustrate him. We'll be there in twenty minutes. Make it as soon after as you can, because I'm busy—"

"Wait a minute! Archie! You're batty. Have you been there? To Ann's apartment?"

"Certainly not. No time—"

"Then where did you get that Roy Douglas?"

"Caught up with him before he got there. No time for explanations. See you Saturday, if not before."

When I got back to the table, the darned fool was having another drink. I called the waiter and paid for it.

Then Roy said, "I can't do it. I can't go. I forgot about my birds. I have to take care of my birds."

Another complication, as if I didn't already have enough to contend with. I got him out of there and into a taxi, and on the way uptown I managed to sell him the idea that I would get in touch with Miss Leeds before 8:00 in the morning and arrange with her to tend the pigeons. The chief trouble now was that he was more than half lit, and what with that and the shock he had had it was a question how much comprehension he had left, so I carefully repeated all the instructions and made sure he knew which pocket the hundred bucks were in.

At that, he seemed to have things fairly under control when we got out at the Ritz. It worked like a charm. We hadn't been waiting more than ten minutes when Lily came out, with only three pieces of luggage, which for her was practically a paper bag. As she waited for the taxi door to be opened I saw her get me out of the corner of her eye, and I handed Roy into another taxi, shook his hand and told him I trusted him, and instructed the driver to hang onto the taxi in front at any cost. I stood and watched them roll off.

My watch said 7:45. I entered the Ritz and sent a telegram to Miss Leeds, signing it Roy Douglas, asking her to take care of my pigeons. I wanted to get back to 35th Street as soon as possible, because it was an open question whether the note I had written to Ann would be discovered by the first squad man that got there, or hours later when the medicals started on the p.m., and I simply had to be home when the phone rang or a visitor arrived. But one little errand had first call, because it was urgent. After all, Roy Douglas was Ann's fiancé, and although it seemed incredible that he could have been coolheaded enough to sit and chin with me about pigeons just after strangling his sweetheart, I had to make sure if I didn't want to make a double-breasted boob of myself. So I went for a phone book and a phone.

It took nearly three-quarters of an hour. First I dialed the number of the National Bird League on the chance that someone might be working late, but there was no answer. Then I went to it. I tried the *Times* and *Gazette*, and finally found someone on the *Herald Tri-*

bune who gave me the name and address of the president of the National Bird League. He lived in Mount Kisco. I phoned there, and he was in Cincinnati, but his wife gave me the name and address of the secretary of the League. I got her, a Brooklyn number, and by gum she had been away from the office that afternoon, attending a meeting, and I had to put all I had on the ball to coax out of her the name and phone number of another woman who worked in the office. At last I had a break; the woman was at home, and apparently bored, for I didn't have to coax her to talk. She worked at the desk next to Ann Amory, and they had left the office together that afternoon at a couple of minutes after five. So it was worth all the trouble, since that was settled. Roy had got to Wolfe's house at 4:55, before Ann had even left the office. It was gratifying to know I hadn't slipped the murderer a hundred bucks to take a trip to the country.

I took a taxi down to 35th Street, stopping on the way to pick up a couple of sandwiches and a bottle of milk, and found that luck was with me there too. All was serene. They had gone to bed. The house was dark. I would have liked to enjoy the sandwiches in the kitchen, but didn't want the doorbell to ring, so I sneaked in and got a glass, turning on no light, and went back to the stoop, closing the door, and sat there on the top step to eat my dinner. Everything was going smooth as silk.

They were pretty good sandwiches. As time wore on I began to get chilly. I didn't want to stamp around on the stoop or pace the sidewalk, since Fritz slept in the basement and I didn't know how soundly he slept during training, so I stood and flapped my arms to work up a circulation. Then I sat on the step again. I looked at my watch and it was 10:40. An hour later I looked again and it was 10:55. Having been afraid before I got there that some squad man might discover the note first thing, now I began to wonder if the damn laboratory was going to wait till morning to start the p.m. and keep me out all night. I stood up and flapped my arms some more.

It was nearly midnight when a police car came zipping down the street and rolled to a stop right in front, and a man got out. I knew him before he hit the sidewalk. It was Sergeant Stebbins of the Homicide Squad. He crossed the sidewalk and started up the steps, and saw me, and stopped.

I said cheerfully, "Hello, Purley. Up so late?"

"Who are you?" he demanded. He peered. "Well, I'll be damned. Didn't recognize you in uniform. When did you get to town?"

"Yesterday afternoon. How's crime?"

"Just fine. What do you say we go in and sit down and have a little conversation?"

"Sorry, can't. Don't talk loud. They're all asleep. I just stepped out for a breath of air. Gee, it's nice to see you again."

"Yeah. I want to ask you a few questions."

"Shoot."

"Well—for instance. When did you last see Ann Amory?"

"Aw, hell," I said regretfully. "You would do that. Ask me the one question I'm not answering tonight. This is my night for not answering any questions whatever about anybody named Ann."

"Nuts," he growled, his bass growl that I had been hearing off and on for ten years. "And I don't mean peanuts. Is it news to you that she's dead? Murdered?"

"Nothing doing, Purley."

"There's got to be something doing. She's been murdered. You know damn well you've got to talk."

I grinned at him. "What kind of got?"

"Well, to start with, material witness. You talk, or I take you down, and maybe I do anyway."

"You mean arrest me as a material witness?"

"That's what I mean."

"Go ahead. It will be the first time I've ever been arrested in the city of New York. And by you! Go ahead."

He growled. He was getting mad. "Goddamn it, Archie, don't be a sap! In that uniform? You're an officer, ain't you?"

"I am. Major Goodwin. You didn't salute."

"Well, for God's sake—"

"No good. Final. Regarding Ann Amory, anything about Ann Amory, I don't open my trap."

"All right," he said. "I've always thought you were cuckoo. You're under arrest. Get in that car."

I did so.

There was one little chore left before I could sit back and let nature take its course. Arriving at Centre Street, and asserting my right to make one phone call, I got a lawyer I knew out of bed and gave him some facts to relay to Bill Pratt of the *Courier*. At 3:45 in the morning, after spending three hours in the company of Inspector Cramer, two lieutenants, and some assorted sergeants and other riffraff, and still refusing to utter a syllable connected in any way with the life or death of Ann Amory, I was locked into a cell in the beautiful new city prison, which is not as beautiful inside as outside.

Chapter 8

It had cost me two bucks to get it smuggled in to me, but it was worth it. Wednesday noon I sat on the edge of my cot in my cell gazing admiringly at it, a front page headline in the early edition of the *Courier:*

ARMY MAJOR HELD IN
MURDER CASE
NERO WOLFE'S FORMER
ASSISTANT LOCKED UP

As the schoolboy said to the teacher, good—hell, it's perfect. The "Army Major" was plenty disgraceful, and the "Nero Wolfe's Former Assistant" was superb. Absolutely degrading. As added attractions, there were pictures of both Wolfe and me on the second page. The article was good too. Bill Pratt hadn't failed me. It gave me a good appetite, so I relinquished another two bucks to send out for a meal that would fit the occasion. After that was disposed of, I stretched out on the cot for a nap, having got behind on my sleep the last two nights.

The opening of the cell door woke me up. I blinked at a guard as he gave me a sign to emerge, rubbed my eyes, stood up, shook myself, enjoyed a yawn, and followed the guard. He led me to an elevator, and, when we got downstairs, through the barrier out of the prison section, then along corridors and into an anteroom, and through that into an office. I had been there before. Except for one object it was familiar: Inspector Cramer at the big desk, Sergeant Stebbins standing near by ready for anything that didn't require mental activity, and a guy with a notebook at a little table at one side. The unfamiliar object, in those surroundings, was Nero Wolfe. He was in a chair by a corner of Cramer's desk, and I had to compress my lips to keep from grinning with satisfaction when I saw that he was no longer dressed for training. He was wearing the dark blue cheviot with a pin stripe, with a yellow shirt and a dark blue tie. Really snappy. The suit didn't fit him any more, but that didn't bother me now.

He looked at me and didn't say a word. But he looked.

Cramer said, "Sit down."

I sat, crossed my legs, and looked surly.

Wolfe took his eyes from me and snapped, "Repeat briefly what you've told me, Mr. Cramer."

"He knows it all," Cramer growled. He had fists on his desk. "At 7:10 last evening Mrs. Chack returned to her apartment at 316 Barnum Street and found her granddaughter, Ann Amory, there on the floor dead, strangled, with a scarf around her neck. A radio car arrived at 7:21, the squad at 7:27, the medical examiner at 7:42. The girl had been dead from one to three hours. The body was removed—"

Wolfe wiggled a finger. "Please. The main points. About Mr. Goodwin."

"He knows them too. Found on the body, underneath the dress, was the note I have shown you, in

Goodwin's handwriting, signed ARCHIE. The paper had been torn from a notebook which was found on his person, now in my possession. Three sets of Goodwin's fingerprints, fresh and recent, were on objects in the apartment. A strand of hair, eleven hairs, found behind the scarf which was around the body's throat, with which she was strangled, has been compared with Goodwin's hair and they match precisely. Goodwin was at that address Monday evening and had an altercation with Mrs. Chack, and took Ann Amory to the Flamingo Club, and left with her hastily on account of a scene with a woman whose name is—not an element in the case. He went to 316 Barnum Street again yesterday and made inquiries of a man named Furey, Leon Furey, and apparently he spent most of the afternoon snooping around the neighborhood. We're still checking that. So the neighborhood is acquainted with him, and two people saw him walking east on Barnum Street, not far from Number 316, between six-thirty and seven o'clock, in company with a man named Roy Douglas, who lives at—"

"That will do," Wolfe snapped. His eyes moved. "Archie. Explain this at once."

"Confronted with this evidence," Cramer rumbled, "Goodwin refuses to talk. He submitted to a search without protest, with that notebook in his pocket. He permitted us to make a microscopic comparison of the strand of hair with his. But he won't talk. And by God," he hit the desk with one of the fists, "you have the gall to come down here, the first time you have ever honored us with a visit, and threaten to have the police department abolished!"

"I merely—" Wolfe began.

"Just a minute!" Cramer roared. "I've been taking your guff for fifteen years, and Goodwin has been riding

for a fall for at least ten. Here it is. He is not now
charged with murder. He is detained as a material
witness. But it's going to take a lot of comedy to laugh
off that strand of hair. It's exactly the kind of thing that
could have happened without him knowing it, the girl
grabbing at him and seizing his hair, and then when he
got the scarf around her, trying to get her fingers
behind it to pull it away and leaving the hair there.
You're smart, Wolfe, as smart a man as I ever knew. All
right, try to figure out any other conceivable way how
Goodwin's hair got behind that scarf. That's why we're
prepared to oppose any application for release on bail."

Cramer pulled a cigar from his pocket, conveyed it
to his mouth, and sank his teeth in it.

"It's all right, boss," I told Wolfe, trying to smile as
if I were trying to smile bravely. "I don't think they'll
ever convict me. I'm pretty sure they can't. I've got a
lawyer coming to see me. You go on home and forget
about it. I don't want you to break training."

Wolfe's lips moved faintly but no sound came out.
He was speechless with rage.

He took a deep breath.

"Archie," he said, "you have the advantage over
me. There is nothing I can do to you. I can't dismiss you,
since you are no longer in my employ." His eyes moved.
"Mr. Cramer, you are an ass. Leave Mr. Goodwin alone
with me for an hour, and I'll get you all the information
you want."

"Alone with you?" Cramer grunted derisively. "Not
that big an ass I'm not."

Wolfe grimaced. He was having all he could do to
control himself.

I said in a manly tone, "It's like this, boss. I'm in a
bad hole. I admit it. I am innocent, but my honor is
involved. A good lawyer may pull me through. I had to

grit my teeth last night to keep from waking you up to tell you about it. I knew you didn't want—"

"Apparently, Archie," he said grimly, "you forget how well I know you. Enough of this flummery. What are your terms?"

He had me flustered for a second. I stammered, "My what? Terms?"

"Yes. For the information I'll have to have to clean up this mess. First to get you out of here. Do you realize, when Fritz brought me that paper and I saw that headline—"

"Yes, sir, I realize. As for terms, it's not me, it's the Army. I'm in it, and I'm on duty. We ask your assistance—"

"You're going to get it. I am preparing for it—"

"Sure you are. You're preparing to dry up and die. We respectfully request an appointment for Colonel Ryder to call on you at the earliest opportunity. We request you to remove your brain from the cedar chest and give me back my sweater, which is stretched out of shape, and go to work."

"Confound you—"

"What the hell," Cramer barked, "is all this?"

"Please be quiet," Wolfe snapped. He folded his arms and shut his eyes, and his lips pushed out and then in again, and out and in. Cramer and I had both seen that before, on various occasions. This time it went on for quite a while. Finally Wolfe heaved a deep sigh and his eyes opened.

"Very well," he muttered at me. "Talk."

I grinned at him. "May I phone Colonel Ryder to come tomorrow at eleven?"

"How do I know? I've got a job to do."

"As soon as it's finished?"

"Yes."

"Okay." I turned to Cramer. "Tell Stebbins to phone Fritz to dust and air the office and to get things in and have dinner at eight, as before—let's see—pan-broiled young turkey and what goes with it. And beer. Three cases of beer."

Purley uttered a grunt of indignation, but Cramer made it an order by nodding at him, and he left the room.

"Also," I told Cramer cheerfully, "before I pull the zipper I want a passport from you. I've got—"

"Save it," he rasped. "It's your turn now. If I like it well enough—"

"Nothing doing." I shook my head firmly. "You're not going to like it at all. Short of murder there's practically nothing you couldn't wrap around me if you felt like it. So I've got terms for you too. You can have the satisfaction of salting me away for ten years—five anyhow. Or you can have the facts. But you're not going to get both satisfaction *and* facts. Now say you lock me up and Mr. Wolfe totters home without me. How long do you think it would take you to find out how a lock of my hair got under that scarf? And so forth. If you want the facts, give me a passport. In advance. And get set to restrain yourself, because I freely admit that in my enthusiasm I—"

"In your what?"

"Enthusiasm. Zeal."

"Yeah."

"Yes, sir. I admit that I acted somewhat arbitrarily and when I tell you about it you will be inclined to take offense. In fact—"

"Don't talk so damn much. What do you want?"

"Fresh air. Short of murder, I'm clear. Not a signed statement, just verbal will do."

"Go to hell."

"Suit yourself." I shrugged. "You can't possibly tag me for murder. I know the facts and you don't. It would take you three thousand years to find out about that lock of hair, let alone—"

"Shut up!"

I did so. Cramer glowered at me, and I gazed at him composedly but inflexibly. Wolfe was leaning back with his eyes closed.

"Okay," he said. "Short of murder you're clear. Shoot."

I stood up. "May I use your phone, please?"

Cramer shoved the phone across and I put in a person-to-person call to Lily Rowan at the Worthington at Greenwich. Evidently she wasn't out leading Roy a chase, for I got her right away. She was inclined to be cantankerous, but I told her all conversation would have to be postponed until I saw her, which would be that very afternoon if she would take the next train to New York and go straight from the station to Wolfe's office. Then I asked her to return me to the hotel switchboard and when I got it asked to speak to Roy Douglas. In a couple of minutes I had him. His voice sounded as if he had the jitters, and he began sputtering about the papers saying he had run away and was being searched for, but I calmed him down and told him the same thing I had told Lily, to return to New York and go to Wolfe's office. When I put the receiver back on the cradle Cramer was regarding me with a mean eye. He reached for the phone and got somebody and growled into it:

"Send four men to Nero Wolfe's place on 35th Street. Lily Rowan and Roy Douglas will be showing up there in a couple of hours, maybe sooner. Let 'em go in Wolfe's house if that's what they do, and keep it covered. If they do anything else, follow them." He hung up and turned to me. "So you had 'em on ice, did you? Both of 'em, huh?" He pointed the cigar at me. "You're wrong about one thing, bud. You won't be seeing any Lily Rowan at Wolfe's office this afternoon, because you're not going to be there. Now let's hear you."

Wolfe muttered, "Talk, Archie."

Chapter 9

I talked. One thing I know how to do is to report current events which I have witnessed, and they both knew it, so there were no interruptions. It didn't present any great difficulties, since all I had to do was open the bag and dump it, as I would have done if I had been alone with Wolfe. I saw no reason to try to hide any cards from Cramer. I gave them the crop, with only one exception. My modesty wouldn't permit me to suggest that reading aloud to me was an essential ingredient in Lily Rowan's life, liberty, and pursuit of happiness, so I skipped any hint of that. I merely said we met by accident on the plane to New York, and she told me about Ann Amory being in trouble, and I decided to try to use that in my effort to bring Nero Wolfe back to his senses. Of course I had to tell about the object of my trip to New York, since otherwise there would have been no way to explain my planting the note and the hair and my fingerprints, and various other details, and anyhow Wolfe already knew it, as he had shown when he asked me what were my terms.

"So," I ended, looking straight at Wolfe, "here I am. I have disgraced the uniform. A million people are at this moment reading the headline, *Nero Wolfe's*

Former Assistant Locked Up, and snickering. Even if Cramer believes my story, he still has a lock of my hair. If he doesn't believe it, he may get me electrocuted. And it's all on account of you! If you—"

Cramer was regarding me sourly, mangling his third cigar, and massaging the back of his neck. "I had a headache," he said cutting me off, "and now it's worse. My son's in Australia with the Air Corps. He's a bombardier."

"I was aware of it," I said politely. "Have you heard from him recently?"

"Go to hell. As you know damn well, Goodwin, I've been wanting to teach you a lesson for years. Here's my chance. Five years would be about right. But short of murder you're clear. I said so, and what I say sticks. If it wasn't for that I'd hang it on you, don't think I wouldn't. Anyway you're wearing the same uniform my son's wearing, and I have more respect for it than you seem to have. And I guess you'll be court-martialed. There was a Colonel Ryder here to see you about an hour ago and I wouldn't let him."

"That'll be all right," I said reassuringly. "As soon as Mr. Wolfe finds the murderer everything will be rosy."

"You don't say. Wolfe's going to find the murderer, is he? That's damn kind of him."

"Archie." Wolfe had found his tongue. "You admit that the sole purpose of this grotesque performance was to bring pressure on me? To coerce me?"

"To stimulate you, yes, sir."

Wolfe nodded grimly. "We'll discuss it at the proper time. I prefer not to do so in the presence of others. First there is this murder. How much of what you told Mr. Cramer was true?"

"All of it."

"You're talking to me now."

"I know I am."

"How much did you withhold?"

"Nothing. That was the works."

"I don't believe it. You hesitated twice."

I shook my head, grinning at him. "You're a little rusty, that's all. You're out of practice. But there is one thing I didn't say. I did want you to get back to work because the Army needs you, but when I saw Ann Amory there on the floor there was another reason. She was a good kid. She was all right. I danced with her and I liked her. If you had seen her as she was Monday evening, and then as she was there on the floor— anyway, I saw her. So I was in favor of making sure that the guy who did it wouldn't live any longer than was necessary, and that was another reason for getting you back to work. Because it may have been partly my fault. I went down there and stirred it up. Otherwise it might not have happened."

"Nonsense," Wolfe said testily. "A murderer doesn't sprout overnight like a mushroom. What about it, Mr. Cramer? What have you got? Do you need anything?"

Cramer grunted. "I didn't need what Goodwin gave me. If I believe him. Say I believe him. I didn't need him to scratch the favorite."

My brows went up. "Roy Douglas? Were you liking him?"

"I was." Cramer tossed the worn-out unlit cigar in the wastebasket. "For one thing, because he beat it. But if I'm believing you, he's good and out. According to three people, the girl left her office a couple of minutes after five. She couldn't have got home before 5:20, probably not before 5:25. Miss Rowan saw her there dead at 5:45, close to that. So she was killed in that twenty minutes. Or even if you want to get fancy and say she was killed somewhere else, as soon as she left the office, and then taken and dumped in the apartment, still Douglas is out. According to you, he got to Wolfe's house before five o'clock and was with you constantly until Miss Rowan arrived."

I nodded. "I told you I checked on her leaving the office. If I had slipped the murderer a hundred bucks for a train ride, that would have been overdoing it. What have you got left? How about Leon Furey?"

"Playing pool at Martin's from four o'clock on. Ate sandwiches there and went on playing. Didn't return to Barnum Street until nearly midnight."

"Sewed up?"

"We thought it was. Now we'll have to go over it. We were after Douglas. We'll have to go back over all of it. I suppose even the grandmother. Two people saw her entering at 7:10, but she could have been there earlier and gone out again. And Miss Leeds. Her agent was with her up to some time between 6:30 and 7:00, going over leases and accounts, and now we'll have to pin that down. We had crossed off four other people who were in the building at the time because they seemed to have no connection with Ann Amory, but we'll have to go back to that too." Cramer glared at me. "Nuts. I don't remember any single time I ever saw you or spoke to you that you didn't ball something up."

He picked up the phone and began giving orders. In ten minutes or less he issued instructions that started a couple of dozen men either going or coming. But I wasn't paying very close attention. In spite of Wolfe's agreeing to see Colonel Ryder and permitting the order to be relayed to Fritz for pan-broiled young turkey, I wasn't sure whether I had him or not. He was as unpredictable as Lily Rowan, and I was trying to figure out some way of getting him really involved. I didn't like the way he looked. He was keeping his eyes open and his head straight up; and there was no way of telling what it meant because it was new to me. Of course the thing to do was to get him home, get him seated back of his desk again, with beer in front of him and smells coming from the kitchen, as soon as possible.

I was considering ways of selling that idea to Cramer, when Cramer saved me the trouble. He pushed the phone aside and said abruptly to Wolfe, "You asked if I need anything. Well, I do. I suppose you've noticed the way things seem to be heading."

"I perceive," Wolfe said dryly, "a general tendency in the direction of Miss Rowan."

Cramer nodded without enthusiasm. "That don't require much perceiving. We've got to go back over everybody, but that's the way it looks now. And Lily Rowan's father was one of my best friends. He got me on the force, and he got me out of a couple of tight holes in the old days when he was on the inside at the Hall. I knew Lily before she could walk. I'm not the man to do any cleaning job on her, and I don't want to turn her over to any of these wolves. I want you to handle her up at your place. And I want to be there in the front room where she can't see me."

Wolfe frowned. "I know her myself. I have given her orchids. She has been pestering me lately. It will not be pleasant." He shot me a glance that was supposed to wither me. Then he regarded Cramer with an expression of repugnance, and heaved a sigh. "Very well. Provided Archie goes with us, and stays. This idiotic farce—"

A dick I didn't know entered the room, advanced at a nod from Cramer and reported: "Mrs. Chack is here and wants to talk. Miss Leeds is with her. Give her to Lieutenant Rowcliff?"

"No," Cramer said, after a glance at the clock, "bring them in here."

Chapter 10

Those two females had been something out of the ordinary when I saw them separately on my first trip to Barnum Street, but marching in that office together they were really something. As far as size and weight went, Miss Leeds could easily have tucked Mrs. Chack under her arm and carried her off, but the expression in Mrs. Chack's black eyes made it seem likely that such things as size and weight would be minor considerations, and age too, if anybody tried to start anything. She had to take two steps to Miss Leeds's one, but she was in front. They were both dressed to sit in a buggy and watch a parade of soldiers returning from the Spanish-American war. When Purley had got them into chairs, Cramer asked, "You ladies have something to say?"

"I have," Mrs. Chack snapped. "I want to know when you are going to get Roy Douglas. I want to see him face to face. He killed my granddaughter."

"You are crazy," Miss Leeds declared huskily but firmly. "You have been crazy for fifty years. I have permitted you to live in my house—"

"I will not tolerate—"

They were both talking at once.

"Ladies!" Cramer boomed. They both stopped talking as if he had turned a valve. "Perhaps," he suggested, "you had better wait outside, Miss Leeds, until I hear what Mrs. Chack has to say—"

"No," Miss Leeds said immovably. "I intend to hear it."

"Then please don't interrupt. You'll get a chance—"

"She has been afraid of me," Mrs. Chack asserted, "since I discovered that her mother poisoned squirrels in Washington Square on December ninth, 1905. That's a prison offense. But now my own granddaughter is dead because I committed a sin myself and have no right to expect the mercy of God and I am willing to be punished. I am old enough to die and I ought to die. When Cora Leeds died on the ninth of December last year I said to myself, in my wretched vanity, it was the Hand of God, because it pleased me. Then when I learned that Roy Douglas had killed Cora Leeds, murdered her, I said I didn't believe it. In my vanity I would not relinquish the Hand of God—"

"Who was Cora Leeds?" Cramer demanded.

"Her mother." Mrs. Chack pointed a bony little finger, straight as an arrow, at Miss Leeds. "I refused—"

"How did you learn that Roy Douglas killed her?"

"Ann told me. My granddaughter. She told me how she knew, but I can't remember. I have been trying to remember since last night. It will come back to me. My mind isn't too old for a thing like that to come back. Cora Leeds was in bed, she had been in bed since she hurt her leg in September, and he put a pillow over her face and held her down, and when she struggled it was too much for her old heart and she died. I think Ann saw him putting the pillow—no, I'm just guessing. You see, I didn't want to remember it because then it wouldn't have been the Hand of God on December ninth, so I forgot it. That's the way an old mind works. Since last night I've been trying to remember so I could come and tell you as soon as I did, but I decided I'd better not wait."

"She's crazy," Miss Leeds stated in her voice like a man. "She has been crazy for—"

Cramer gestured her into silence without taking his gaze away from Mrs. Chack. "But," he rumbled, "you said that Roy Douglas killed your granddaughter. Do you remember how you know that?"

"Certainly I do," she snapped. "He killed her because she knew he had killed Cora Leeds, and he was afraid of her. He was afraid she would tell someone. Isn't that a good reason?"

"Yeah, it's all right for a reason. Have you got any proof? Any evidence? Did you see him around there?"

"See him? How could I? I wasn't there. When I got home she was dead." Her voice got shrill. "I am eighty-nine years old! I went home and found my granddaughter dead! Could I sit right down and think it out? After I was in bed I knew he had killed her! I want you to get him! I want to see him face to face!"

"You will," Cramer assured her. "Take it easy, Mrs. Chack. Do you remember why he killed Cora Leeds?"

"Certainly I do. Because he didn't want to give up his pigeon loft. She was going to have it torn down."

"I thought she had built it for him," I put in.

"She had. She spent thousands of dollars on it. But after she hurt her leg and couldn't go to the Square any more, she hated him and she hated everybody. She sent word to me that I had to move out, had to leave that house where I had lived for over forty years. And she told Leon he had to get out and she wouldn't pay him any more for killing hawks. She had paid him twenty dollars for every hawk he killed. And she told Roy

Douglas she owned the pigeons, he didn't, and she was going to tear the loft down and he had to go. And she told her own daughter she had to stop going to the Square, and when she found out her daughter was secretly giving money to Leon for killing hawks she wouldn't let her have any money for anything. That's the way she acted after she hurt her leg and couldn't go to the Square. It was no wonder I thought it was the Hand of God, especially when it happened on December ninth. But God forgive me, it wasn't. And I knew it wasn't, I knew it was Roy Douglas, because Ann told me—God forgive me."

Cramer cleared his throat and asked, "From what you said, Miss Leeds, I understand you don't agree with Mrs. Chack?"

"I do not," Miss Leeds declared emphatically. "She's crazy. She did it herself."

"Did what herself? Made that up?"

"No, she did it. She killed my mother and she killed her granddaughter. I doubt if she even knows she did it. Nobody in their right mind would have hurt Ann. She was a nice child and everybody liked her."

"Excuse me," I put in. "You told me Monday that nobody killed your mother. You said she died of old age. Now you say—"

"And you said," she retorted crushingly, "that you came there just to see Ann, and here you are. Didn't I tell you, Army or police, it's all the same? Here you are together, and what do you do about anything? In sixty years you haven't moved a finger to stop the hawks entering the city. What was the sense of my telling you that that crazy old woman killed my mother? What would you have done about it? How did I know she was going to kill Ann too? I only came with her because—"

"Madam!" Wolfe said in a tone that stopped her. "If

you yourself are sane, you can answer a question. Did your mother tell Mrs. Chack to leave the house?"

"Yes. It was her house—"

"Did she stop paying Leon Furey for killing hawks and tell him to leave also?"

"Yes. After she got hurt—"

"Did she tell Roy Douglas she was going to tear down his pigeon loft?"

"Yes. She couldn't bear—"

"Did she quit giving you money and forbid you to go to the Square?"

"Yes. But I didn't—"

"Then, madam, your diagnosis is faulty. Mrs. Chack's mind retains all those details with accuracy, which is a creditable performance at her age. I wouldn't advise you—"

The phone buzzed and Cramer took it. He listened briefly, said to wait, and spoke to Wolfe, "I'm through if you are." Wolfe nodded, and Cramer told the phone, "Come and escort the ladies out and then bring him in."

Escorting the ladies out wasn't so simple. They weren't through, whether Wolfe and Cramer were or not. Finally Cramer had to leave his desk to get them herded through the door, and by the time he got back to his chair in came a city employee with another visitor.

Chapter 11

Leon Furey wasn't liking himself as well as he had been the last time I saw him. As he walked in, looked around at us, and dropped into a chair by invitation, he was not jaunty. It was doubtful if he had been in his pajamas until noon that day, because his clothes looked as if he had not taken them off at all. Sizing him up as he sat there, with lumps under his bloodshot eyes and a two-day growth of beard, I saw nothing inconsistent with the theory that he had tied that scarf around Ann Amory's throat, except the alibi, and that didn't show.

"You want to say something?" Cramer asked.

"Yes, I do." Leon spoke too loud for a man out in the clear and really satisfied with the surroundings. "I want to know why you've got men following me. I've been absolutely straight on this and I've accounted for every minute of my time, and you've verified it. What right have you got to treat me like a criminal? Having me followed, checking up on my draft registration, investigating everywhere I've been and everything I've done for God knows how long. What's the big idea?"

"Routine in a murder case," Cramer said shortly.

"We waste a lot of time that way. If you're claiming injury, get a lawyer. Is it pinching you somewhere?"

"That's not the question." Leon's voice stayed loud. "I've proved that I had nothing to do with any murder, you know damn well I have, and you've got no right to go on investigating me as if I might have had. And I've got a right to make a living the same as anybody. Doing it by killing hawks may or may not meet with your approval, but if Miss Leeds wants to pay me for it what business is it of yours or anybody else's?"

Cramer grunted. "Oh, that's it."

"Yes, that's it. Wasting the taxpayer's money telephoning all over the state of New York. All right, so you find out that farmers have been shipping me hawks they shot and I've been paying them five dollars per hawk. So what? Is that a crime? If Miss Leeds is willing to cough up twenty dollars for a dead hawk, and that gives me a little profit for my trouble, does that make it a crime? It made her happy, didn't it? Hawks are destructive. They kill chickens. My plan benefits the state, it benefits the farmers, it benefits Miss Leeds, it benefits me, and it hurts nobody."

"Then what are you beefing about?"

"I'm beefing because I think you're going to tell Miss Leeds about it, and that would put me out of business. If it so happens that she has got the impression that the hawks are killed right here in New York City, and that gives her pleasure, what's that to you? Or to me either? What it amounts to, in its simplest terms, I'm doing her a favor. And I'm not hogging it. I keep it down to an average of three or four a week. I could make it twice or three times that if I—"

"Beat it." Cramer growled in disgust. "Get the hell out of here. I don't— Wait a minute. You organized this dead hawk business quite a while ago, didn't you?"

"Why—no, I wouldn't say—"

"How long ago?"

Leon hesitated. "I don't remember exactly."

"Say a year ago?"

"Why, yes, sure, at least a year ago."

"What did old Mrs. Leeds pay you? Same as her daughter does? Twenty dollars per hawk?"

"That's right. She set the figure, I didn't."

"And after she hurt her leg and had to stay in bed she refused to pay you any more? And wouldn't let her daughter pay you? And ordered you to move out?"

"Oh, that." Leon waved it away contemptuously.

"Was that because she found out that you weren't killing the hawks, as you said you were, but were collecting them from farmers?"

"It was not. It was because she couldn't enjoy life any more and didn't want anyone else to. How could she have found out about the hawks? She was laid up in bed."

"I'm asking you."

"And I've answered you." Leon leaned forward. "What I want to know is, are you going to ruin my business or not? You've got no right—"

"Take him away," Cramer said wearily. "Stebbins! Take him away!"

Sergeant Stebbins performed.

With the company gone, the three of us looked at one another. I yawned. Wolfe was letting his shoulders sag. He was already forgetting to keep them straight. Cramer got out a cigar, scowled at it, and stuck it back in his pocket.

"Thoughtful of them," Wolfe said conversationally. "To come and tell you things like that."

"Yeah." Cramer was massaging the back of his neck. "That was a big help. There's a precinct report on the death of old Mrs. Leeds and all it's good for is scrap paper. Say they did all have a motive to get rid of her. Then what? Where does that get me on the murder of Ann Amory? With the alibis they've got. And Mrs. Chack's story about what she can't remember that her granddaughter told her about Roy Douglas. That's just fine. With Goodwin here claiming that Douglas was with him at the only time it could have happened." He glared at me. "Look, son, I've known you to put over some fast ones; you know I have. By God, if you're covering up on Douglas I don't care if you're a brigadier general—"

"I'm not," I told him firmly. "I'm not covering up on anyone or anything. You're not going to pass the buck to me. Here you are, the head of the New York Homicide Squad and the great and only Nero Wolfe, and apparently the best you can do with a murder case is to sit and wonder whether I'm a liar or not. Well, I'm not. Cross that off and go to work. Douglas is out. I did that much for you last night on the telephone. Forget him. You say Leon Furey's alibi stands up. Then forget him too. In my opinion, if you want it, Miss Leeds and Mrs. Chack are also out. I knew that girl, and I don't believe either of those women strangled her. So all you've got left is the population of the city of New York, between seven and eight million—"

"Including," Cramer growled, "Lily Rowan."

"By all means," I agreed, "include her. I don't pretend I would open a bottle of milk to celebrate her going to the electric chair, but whoever did that to Ann Amory isn't getting any discount from me. If it was Lily Rowan, you don't have to worry about means and opportunity. She admits she was there, and so was the scarf; I suppose you know it was Ann's. So dig up a motive for her, and you're set."

"A motive would help." Cramer was eyeing me. "Up at the Flamingo Club Monday night. It's hard to get anything definite from that bunch, but the impression seems to be that she was getting ready to throw the furniture at you when you ran. Taking the Amory girl with you. Was she sore because she was jealous? Was she jealous of Ann Amory? Was she jealous enough to go down there the next day and lose her temper? I'm asking."

I shook my head. "You're flattering me, Inspector. I don't arouse passions like that. It's my intellect women like. I inspire them to read good books, but I doubt if I could inspire even Lizzie Borden to murder. You can forget the Flamingo Club. It wasn't even a tiff. You say you know Lily Rowan. She had given me the tip on Ann Amory being in trouble, as I've told you, and she was sore because I was following it up without letting her in on it. You'll have to do better on motive than that. I'm not saying—"

The phone rang. Cramer answered it, listened a minute, grunted instructions, pushed the phone back, and stood up.

"They're there," he announced. "Both of them. Let's go." He didn't look happy. "You handle her, Wolfe. I don't want to see her until I have to."

Chapter 12

The trouble was, I couldn't enjoy it.

It was okay again, and it was my doing. The office was dusted and tidied up. Wolfe was in his made-to-order chair back of his desk. There was a bottle of beer in front of him. Faint sounds could be heard of Fritz busy in the kitchen. I had done it in less than 48 hours. But I couldn't enjoy it. First, on account of Ann Amory. I had gone to see her with the big idea of getting Wolfe to get her out of trouble, and what had happened—well, I had got her out of trouble, all right. She wasn't ever going to have any more trouble.

Second, Lily Rowan. Without trying to analyze all my feelings about her, it was a cinch there was nothing attractive in the notion of helping to send her up the river, to be taken down the corridor on a summer night to sit in the chair that nobody ever sits in more than once. On the other hand, if she had gone completely haywire, or maybe had some reason I didn't know about, and had pulled that scarf around Ann's neck, I couldn't say I didn't want that to happen. I did want it to happen. But the net result of things was that I wasn't enjoying any triumph at seeing the office back in commission again.

I had supposed that Wolfe would take them separately, but he didn't. I was at my desk with my notebook. Roy Douglas was seated off to my right, facing Wolfe, and Lily was in the red leather chair near the other end of Wolfe's desk. The door to the front room was open, and around the corner, out of sight, Cramer and Stebbins were planted. Lily and Roy didn't know they were there. Another thing that was eating me was the expression on Lily's face and the way she was acting. The way she had spoken to Wolfe and me. There was that little twist to a corner of her mouth, so slight that it had taken me a year to get onto it, that was there when she was betting the stack on four spades with nothing but a six of clubs in the hole. It made her look cocky and made you feel that she was so sure of herself that you might as well quit. Even when you knew about it, you had to be careful not to let it take you in.

Wolfe was as exasperating as I had ever heard him—I mean exasperating to me. But I understood it, or thought I did; it was a war of nerves with Lily, who had to sit there and listen to it. He asked Roy about the loft, the pigeons, how he had first met Miss Leeds and her mother, Mrs. Chack, Ann, Leon Furey, how often had he been in the Chack-Amory apartment, how long had he lived at 316 Barnum Street, where did he live before that, how well did he know Lily Rowan, and on around the mulberry bush. As time dragged on he got my notebook filled with sixteen bushels of useless facts. Neither Leon nor Roy paid any rent for their rooms, Roy had been up on the roof exercising pigeons the afternoon old Mrs. Leeds had died, and had learned about it from Leon when he came down at dark. The upkeep of the loft amounted to around $4,000 a year, including purchase of new birds. About half of it came from prize money and the rest from Miss Leeds, formerly from her mother. Mrs. Leeds had threatened to tear the loft down, Roy admitted that, but then she was threatening everybody with everything, including her own daughter, and no one took it seriously. Roy had not known Lily Rowan. He had heard Ann mention her, that was about all. He couldn't remember that Ann had ever said anything special about her.

No, he said, Ann had not told him what kind of trouble she was in, or who or what it was about, but from the way she acted he knew something was worrying her. My coming to take Ann to see Lily Rowan on Monday, and my coming back the next day to see him, had made him curious, and since he and Ann were engaged to be married he felt he had a right to know what was going on, so he came to ask me about it. He insisted that was the only reason he came to see me. He had no idea at all that Ann was in danger, and certainly no urgent danger like someone wanting to kill her, and he had no notion who had done it or why. He was sure it couldn't have been anybody at 316 Barnum Street, because they all liked her, even Leon Furey, who was cynical about everything.

At 5:20 Lily Rowan said, "Don't talk so loud, Roy. You'd better whisper. You might wake him up."

I was inclined to agree with her. Wolfe was leaning back comfortably in his chair, his arms folded, with his eyes closed, and I had a suspicion that he was about two-thirds asleep. He had finished two bottles of beer, after going without for over a month, and he was back in the only chair in the world he liked, and his insane project of going outdoors and walking fast twice a day was only a hideous memory.

He heaved a deep sigh and half opened his eyes, with their focus on Lily.

"It is no occasion for drollery, Miss Rowan," he

muttered at her. "Especially for you. You are suspected of murder. At a minimum that is nothing to be jocund about."

"Ha," she said. She didn't laugh; she merely said, "Ha."

Wolfe shook his head. "I assure you, madam, it is not a time to ha. The police suspect you. They will annoy you and irritate you. They will ask questions of your friends and enemies. They will dig into your past. They will do it poorly, without any discrimination, and that will make it worse. They will go back as far as they can, for they know that Miss Amory's father worked for your father a long while ago, and they will surmise— probably they already have—that the reason for your killing Miss Amory is buried in that old association." Wolfe's shoulders went up a quarter of an inch and settled back again. "It will be extremely disagreeable. So I suggest that we clear it away now, all that we can of it."

The twist was at the corner of Lily's mouth. "I think," she said, "that you and Archie ought to be ashamed of yourselves. I thought you were friends of mine, and here you are trying to prove I committed murder. When I didn't." She switched to me, "Archie, look at me. Look in my eyes. Really I didn't, Archie."

Wolfe wiggled a finger at her. "You went to that apartment yesterday afternoon to see Miss Amory, arrived about 5:40 or 5:45, found the door open, walked in, and saw her there on the floor, dead. Is that it?"

Lily studied him, with her forehead wrinkled. "I don't believe," she said slowly, "that I'm going to talk about it. Of course I'd be willing to discuss it with you as a friend, but this is different."

"I am merely repeating what you told Mr. Goodwin."

"Then there's no use going over it again, is there?"

Wolfe's eyes opened the rest of the way. He was beginning to get riled. "I am going on the assumption," he said testily, "that you either killed Miss Amory or you didn't, which seems reasonable. If you did, the way you conduct yourself here is strictly your own affair. If you didn't you are foolish to act in a way that enforces suspicion of you. It would be a good plan for you to give the impression that you are willing to help us find out who killed Miss Amory, in either case."

"I am perfectly willing. More than willing. I'm anxious. But this is a fine way to go about it. Keeping me sitting here for hours while you pump this Roy Douglas." Lily was indignant. "Cops in front of the house. That room probably full of cops. Starting out by telling me I'm suspected of murder. Archie taking down what I say." She turned on me. "You bum, this is a swell way to repay me for obeying orders the way I did! I never took orders from anyone else in my life and you know it!"

She went back to Wolfe. "As far as Ann Amory is concerned, if Archie has told you what I told him, you know all I know. I hadn't seen her or thought of her for years until she came to see me a few weeks ago and said she was in trouble and wanted me to send her to a lawyer. All I can do is repeat what I told Archie."

"Do so," Wolfe muttered.

"I will not! Let him do it!" She was warming up. She turned on me again:

"Look at you, you damn stenographer! Telling me to come here and talk it over, and this is what I run into! I used to have some sense until I met you! Now what do I do ? Chase off down to Washington just to find out where you are because you won't answer my telegrams! Use enough pull to get my picture on the cover of *Life* just to find you're taking an airplane and get a seat on it! Not only that, blab it all out to you because it might soften your heart! And you were too busy to make any social engagements, and I phone here fifty times, and finally I go out for a drink, and there you are dancing! If I ever do go in for murder, I know exactly where I'll start! And on top of all that I'm enough of a sap to pack up and take a train—"

"Please!" Wolfe said peremptorily. "Miss Rowan!"

She sat back. "There," she said in a tone of satisfaction, "I feel better. I wanted to get that off my chest in the presence of witnesses. Now if you'll instruct him to take me somewhere and buy me a drink—"

"Please," Wolfe said curtly, "don't get started again. I sympathize with your resentment at the presence of the police, but it's not my fault. None of this is my fault. I abandon any attempt to question you about Miss Amory, but I would like to ask you one or two things about Mr. Goodwin. Apparently you find him as vexatious as I do. Did I understand you to say that you went to Washington in search of him, and went to some trouble to get a seat on the airplane he was taking, and informed him of that fact?"

"Yes."

"On Monday? Day before yesterday?"

"Yes."

"Indeed." Wolfe pursed his lips. "He said that meeting was accidental. I didn't know he had a streak of modesty in him."

"I wouldn't worry about it," Lily said sarcastically. "He hasn't. He wouldn't think it was worth bragging about unless it was the three Soong sisters."

Wolfe nodded. "It's only that it gives me an idea. You say he hadn't answered your telegrams. Possibly your pestering—that is, your recent efforts to communicate with me came from your desire, not so much to help Miss Amory as to learn the whereabouts of Mr. Goodwin. If you would care to answer that—"

"They did."

"I see. And the phone ringing here Monday evening, that was you. And Tuesday? Yesterday? Was that also you?"

"Yes. You might as well—"

"Please. I can guess what all that frustration might have done to a woman of your temperament. It is only a guess, but it deserves a little investigation." Wolfe raised his voice. "Mr. Cramer! Come here, please!"

By the time we got our heads turned Cramer was in the doorway.

"I knew it," Lily said. "I knew darned well there were cops in there. But I didn't know it was you. What do you think Dad would think of that?"

"I believe you know Miss Rowan," Wolfe said. "I've got a little job for Sergeant Stebbins and those men out in front." He paused. "No, the Sergeant had better stay here. Are those men any good?"

"Medium," Cramer rumbled. "What—"

"They ought to do for this. Send them up to the Ritz. To interview Miss Rowan's maid, elevator men, bellboys, the doormen, telephone girls, everybody. We want to know, to the minute if possible, what time Miss Rowan left there Tuesday afternoon. Especially if it was late in the afternoon, say approaching six o'clock—Did you wish to say something, Miss Rowan?"

"No," Lily said. She was gawking at him incredulously.

"Very well. Of course you may have left the Ritz at any time during the afternoon, I realize that. But other inquiries can be made. Whether, for instance, Miss Amory received a phone call at her office that afternoon. Whether the bell of any of the tenants at 316 Barnum Street rang between 5:30 and 5:45. Whether—"

"My God," Lily said. "You actually did guess it!"

"Indeed," Wolfe said quietly. His eyes had a glint in them. "Then you might as well save us the trouble. What time did you leave the Ritz on Tuesday?"

"A little before six. About a quarter to. You know, if I was as smart as you are—"

"Thank you. And came straight here?"

"Yes."

Wolfe grunted and turned his head. "Sergeant? Over here. There's your man. Roy Douglas. You can arrest him for the murder of Ann Amory."

We all moved, to stare at Roy, but he didn't because he was frozen. He sat stiff, rigid, gaping at Wolfe.

"Hold it, Stebbins," Cramer growled. He moved alongside Roy and kept his eyes on him, but spoke to Wolfe. "We don't charge men with murder just on your say-so, Wolfe. Suppose you fill it in."

"My dear sir," Wolfe said petulantly. "Isn't it obvious? Miss Rowan just said she left the Ritz at 5:45 Tuesday and came straight here. Therefore she didn't go to Barnum Street at all. She invented that tale about finding Miss Amory dead in her apartment, with a scarf around her neck, because she was determined to see Archie, and, being a female, is utterly irresponsible—"

"You go to the devil," Lily told him. "I only said that to get him to let me in, I didn't know anyone else was there, I wanted him to come and have a drink, and then the way he took it, it went over so big—"

"She must have gone to Barnum Street," Cramer insisted doggedly. "She described it to Goodwin, the body there on the floor propped against a chair with a scarf around her neck—"

"I didn't do it!" Roy whined. He was trying to stand up, but Cramer had a hand on his shoulder. "I tell you I didn't do it! I tell you I didn't—"

"I'm not going to tolerate much of that," Wolfe said grimly.

Cramer held Roy down in the chair. Roy was starting to tremble. Cramer was going on, "How the hell could she describe it if she hadn't seen it—" He chopped it off. "Oh, I'll be damned!"

"Certainly," Wolfe said impatiently. "That's the point. She described it, and he heard her. It was good news for him, the best possible news, since it ended his fear that Miss Amory would disclose her knowledge that he had murdered Mrs. Leeds, but naturally he was startled, and had no idea who had done the job for him."

"I didn't!" Roy was whining. "I didn't do it—"

"Shut up!" Cramer barked at him.

"So," Wolfe went on, "he dashed down there as fast as he could, and was disconcerted to find that Miss Amory was not quite dead enough. Not, of course, dead at all. Alive and well. His mortification turned him into an imbecile. He conceived the silliest idea in the history of crime. He strangled her with a scarf and propped her up against a chair, the idea being that since Miss Rowan had already described the scene as he arranged it, he had an alibi that could not be broken. I don't know when he realized how idiotic that was; anyway, when it was done it was done, and Archie arrived so promptly that he had no time to realize anything."

"I didn't—" Roy was trembling all over, and trying to squirm out of Cramer's grasp, but Stebbins had his other shoulder and was getting out handcuffs for him.

Wolfe grimaced and went on. "Of course, instead of saving him, his gambit condemns him. Since it can be proven that Miss Amory left her office after five o'clock, and that Miss Rowan left the Ritz at 5:45 and arrived here ten minutes later, Miss Rowan couldn't possibly have seen what she said she did at Miss Amory's apartment, and therefore her description of that scene was an invention. Also Miss Rowan will herself testify to that; she'll have to. But since the scene actually was as she described it, the inexorable conclusion is that it was staged by someone who heard her describe it. That alone will convict him."

I started to say something, but found I had no voice. I cleared my throat and got it out, "I heard her describe it too, you know."

"Pfui." Wolfe was scornful. "With all your defects, Archie, you are neither a strangler nor a nincompoop." He wiggled a finger at Cramer. "Get that wretch out of here."

Chapter 13

An hour later, around half past seven, Wolfe and I were alone in the office. He was behind his desk, with the atlas opened at the map of Australia, and every now and then he lifted his head to sniff. The turkey was broiling in the kitchen.

I reached for the phone and tried again, the third time, for Colonel Ryder at Governor's Island. He wasn't there but was expected back any minute.

"I would like to say," I told Wolfe, "that you are wrong about Ann Amory being a sentimental imbecile for not telling the police as soon as she learned that Roy had killed Mrs. Leeds. I knew her and you didn't. I doubt if she really knew Roy had done it, I mean actually saw it. My guess is she saw something that gave her a strong suspicion. She told Mrs. Chack about it, but Mrs. Chack talked her out of it."

Wolfe muttered, "Imbecile."

"No," I said with conviction. "She was a damn good kid. I tell you I knew her. Mrs. Chack nearly talked her out of it, but not quite, and it kept worrying her. After all, she was engaged to marry the guy. I'm betting she put it up to him straight, that would have been like her, and of course he denied it, but that didn't convince her either, and then he was afraid she might spill it to someone any minute, and he probably acted queer—he would—and that made her suspicion stronger. Of course she knew he had had plenty of motive. The only thing he cared about in the world was that loft and the damn pigeons, and Mrs. Leeds was going to take them away from him and kick him out. But she wasn't absolutely sure he had done it. Nice situation. She couldn't just let it ride, but she didn't want to denounce him to the police. So she tried to get expert advice by asking Lily Rowan to send her to a lawyer. She was trying to do it right. She wouldn't even tell me about it. But when I bounced in down there he got scared good and proper. And she would have told you. That is, she would if you had been approachable."

"Imbecile," Wolfe muttered.

There was no question about his being back to normal. Me too. He gave me a pain in the neck. But being in uniform and on duty, I had to suppress my personal emotions. I reached for the phone and dialed the number again, and this time got him. As soon as he heard my name he began to sputter, but I ignored it.

"Colonel Ryder," I said stiffly, "an appointment has been arranged for you with Mr. Nero Wolfe at eleven o'clock tomorrow morning, if you will kindly be at his office at that hour. If you will arrive at ten-thirty, I shall be glad to furnish you with an explanation of the unfortunate publicity I received today, which I feel sure will be satisfactory. At that time I shall also explain why it will be necessary for me to have a week-end leave beginning Saturday noon. My word of honor as an officer is involved."

As I hung up Wolfe raised his head for another sniff of the aroma from the kitchen. My own mind was concentrated on something else. I was permitted some latitude in my expense account, but to make an entry, *Sending murderer on trip to country, $100,* seemed inadvisable. My solution of the problem is a military secret.

Chapter 1

On our way out of the house—his house, which was also his office, on West 35th Street over near the North River—Nero Wolfe, who was ahead of me, stopped so abruptly that I nearly bumped into him. He wheeled and confronted me, glancing at my briefcase.

"Have you got that thing?"

I looked innocent. "What thing?"

"You know very well. That confounded grenade. I want that infernal machine out of this house. Have you got it?"

I held my ground. "Colonel Ryder," I said in a crisp military tone, "who is my superior officer, said I could keep it for a souvenir in view of my valor and devotion to duty in recovering—"

"You can't keep it in my house. I tolerate pistols as a tool of the business, but not that contraption. If by accident the pin got removed it would blow off the top of the building, not to mention the noise it would make. I thought you understood this is out of discussion. Get it, please."

Formerly I might have argued that my room on the third floor was my castle, tenanted by me as part of my pay for suffering his society as his assistant and guardian, but that was out now, since Congress was taking care of me by appropriating around ten billion bucks a month. So I merely shrugged to show I was humoring him, and, knowing how it annoyed him to be kept waiting standing up, moseyed over to the stair and took my time mounting the two flights to my room. It was there where I kept it on top of the chest of drawers—about seven inches long and three in diameter, painted a pale pink, looking nothing like as deadly as it was supposed to be. Reaching for it, I glanced at the safety pin to make sure it was snug, put it in the briefcase, went back downstairs at my leisure, ignored a remark he saw fit to make, and accompanied him out to the curb where the sedan was parked.

One thing Wolfe demanded from the Army, and got, was enough gas for his car. Not that he was trying to bypass the war. He really was making sacrifices for victory. As one, most of his accustomed income from the detective business. Two, his daily sessions with his orchids in the plant rooms on the roof, whenever Army work interfered. Three, his fixed rule to avoid the hazards of unessential movements, especially outdoors. Four, food. I kept an eye on that, looking for a chance to insert remarks, and drew a blank. He and Fritz accomplished wonders within the limitations of coupon fodder, and right there in the middle of New York, with black markets tipping the wink like floozies out for a breath of air on a summer evening, Wolfe's kitchen was as pure as cottage cheese.

After burning up not more than half a gallon of the precious gas, even counting traffic stops and starts, I let him out in front of 17 Duncan Street, found a place to park, and walked back and joined him in the lobby.

Leaving the elevator at the tenth floor, Wolfe had a chance to suppress some more irritation. In my uniform all I had to do was return the salute of the corporal on guard, but although Wolfe had been there at least a couple dozen times and it was no trick to recognize him, he was in cits, and the New York headquarters of Military Intelligence was finicky about civilian visitors. After he got the high sign we went through a door, down a long corridor with closed doors on both sides, one of which was to my office, turned a corner, and entered the anteroom of the Second in Command.

An Army sergeant was sitting at a desk giving the keyboard of a typewriter the one-two.

I said good morning.

"Good morning, Major," the sergeant replied. "I'll tell them you're here." She reached for a phone.

Wolfe was staring. "What in the name of heaven is this?" he demanded.

"WAC," I told him. "We've got some new furniture since you were here last. Brightens the place up."

He compressed his lips and continued to stare. Nothing personal; what was eating him was the sight of a female, in uniform, in that job.

"It's all right," I soothed him. "We don't tell her any of the important secrets, such as Captain So-and-So wears a corset."

She was through at the phone. "Colonel Ryder said to ask you to join them, sir."

I said sternly, "You didn't salute."

If she'd had a sense of humor she'd have stood up and snapped one at me, but in the ten days she had been there I hadn't been able to discover any sign of it. Which didn't mean I had quit trying. I had decided she was putting it on. Her serious efficient eyes and straight functional nose led you to expect a jutting bony chin, but that's where she fooled you. It didn't jut. It would have fitted nicely in the palm of your hand if things ever got to that point.

She was speaking. "I beg your pardon, Major Goodwin. I am obeying the regulations—"

"Okay." I waved it aside. "This is Mr. Nero Wolfe. Sergeant Dorothy Bruce of the United States Army."

They acknowledged each other. Stepping to a door at the other end, I opened it, let Wolfe go through, then followed him and shut the door.

It was a roomy corner office with windows on two sides and the space of the other two walls filled with locked steel cabinets reaching two-thirds of the way to the ceiling, except for a spot occupied by another door which gave access to the hall without going through the anteroom.

There was no humor in there either. The four men on chairs were about as chipper as a bunch of Dodger fans after watching dem bums drop a double-header. Seeing that the atmosphere didn't call for military etiquette, I let the arm hang. The two colonels and the lieutenant we knew, and though we had never met the civilian we knew who he was, having been told about him; and besides, almost any good citizen would have recognized John Bell Shattuck. He was shorter than I would have expected, and maybe a little bulkier, but there was no mistaking his manner as he got up to shake hands with us and look us in the eye. True, we were residents of New York, but an elected person can never be sure you aren't going to move to his own state and be a constituent with a vote.

"Meeting Nero Wolfe is a real occasion," he said, in a voice that sounded as if it was pitched lower than God intended it to be. I had run across that before. Half the statesmen in Washington have been trying to sound like Winston Churchill ever since he made that speech to Congress.

Wolfe was polite to him and then turned back to Ryder. "This is my first opportunity, Colonel, to offer my condolences. Your son. Your only son."

Ryder's jaw was set. It had been for nearly a week, since the news came. "Yes," he said. "Thank you."

"Had he killed any Germans?"

"He had shot down four German planes. Presumably he killed Germans. I hope he did."

"No doubt." Wolfe grunted. "I can't speak about him, I didn't know him. I know you. I would hold up your heart if I could. Obviously you are capable of holding your chin up yourself." He looked around at the chairs that were empty, saw they were of equal dimensions, and moved to one and got himself onto it, with the usual lapping over at the edges. "Where was it?"

"Sicily," Ryder said.

"He was a fine boy," John Bell Shattuck put in. "I was his godfather. No finer boy in America. I was proud of him. I still am proud of him."

Ryder closed his eyes, opened them again, reached for the phone on his desk, and spoke in it. "General Fife." After a moment he spoke again, "Mr. Wolfe has come, General. We're all here. Shall we come up now? Oh. Very well, sir. I understand."

He pushed the phone back and told the room, "He's coming here."

Wolfe grimaced, and I knew why. He knew there was a bigger chair up in the general's office, in fact two of them. I moved to Ryder's desk, put my briefcase on it, unbuckled the straps, and took out the grenade.

"Here, Colonel," I said, "I might as well do this while we're waiting. Where shall I put it?"

Ryder scowled at me. "I said you could keep it."

"I know, but I have no place to keep it except my room at Mr. Wolfe's house, and that won't do. I caught him tinkering with it last night. I'm afraid he'll hurt himself."

Everybody looked at Wolfe. He said testily, "You know Major Goodwin, don't you? I wouldn't touch the thing. Nor will I have it on my premises."

I nodded regretfully. "So the cat came back."

Ryder picked it up and glanced at the safety, saw it was secure, and then suddenly he was out of his chair and on his feet, straight as a Rockette, as the door opened and Sergeant Dorothy Bruce's voice came to us, clipped and military: "General Fife!"

When the general had entered she backed out again, taking the door along. Of course by that time the rest of us were Rocketteing too. He returned our salute, crossed to shake hands and exchange greetings with John Bell Shattuck, and, after another sharp glance around, stretched an arm and pointed a finger at Ryder's left hand.

"What the devil are you doing with that thing?" he demanded. "Playing catch?"

Ryder's hand came up holding the grenade. "Major Goodwin just returned it, sir."

"Isn't it one of those H14's?"

"Yes, sir. As you know, he found them. I gave him permission to keep one."

"You did? I didn't. Did I?"

"No, sir."

Ryder opened a drawer of his desk, put the grenade in it, and closed the drawer. General Fife went to a chair and twirled it around and sat on it assbackwards, crossing his arms along the top of the chair's back. The understanding was that he had formed that habit after seeing a picture of Eisenhower sitting like that, which I record without prejudice. He was the only professional soldier in the bunch there present. Colonel Ryder had been a lawyer out in Cleveland. Colonel Tinkham, who looked like a collection of undersized features put together at random in order to have somewhere to stick a little brown mustache, had had some kind of a gumshoe job for a big New York bank. Lieutenant Lawson had just come up from Washington two weeks before and was still possibly mysterious personally, but not ancestrally. He was Kenneth Lawson, Junior; Senior being the Eastern Products Corporation tycoon who had served his country in its hour of need by lopping one hundred thousand dollars off his own salary. All I really knew about Junior was that I had heard him trying to date Sergeant Bruce his second day in the office and getting turned down.

The only chair left was over by the steel cabinets, occupied by a small pigskin suitcase. Trying to make just the right amount of noise and commotion for a major under the circumstances, I deposited the suitcase on the floor and sat down.

Meanwhile General Fife was speaking. "Where have you got to? Where's the public? Where's the press? No photographers?"

Lieutenant Lawson started to grin, caught Colonel Ryder's eye, and composed his handsome features. Colonel Tinkham moved the tip of his forefinger along the grain of his mustache, right and left alternately, which was his number-one gesture for conveying the impression that he was quite unperturbed.

"We haven't got anywhere, sir," Ryder said. "We

haven't started. Wolfe just got here. Your other questions—"

"Not for you," Fife said curtly. He was looking, conspicuously, at John Bell Shattuck. "Public servant, and no public? No microphones? No newsreel cameras? How are the people to be informed?"

Shattuck didn't even blink, let alone try to return the punch. "Now look here," he said reproachfully, "we're not as bad as that. We try to do our duty, and so do you. Sometimes I think it might be a good plan for us to take over the armed forces for a period, say a month—"

"Good God."

"—and let the generals and admirals take over the Capitol for the same period. No doubt we would all learn something. I assure you I understand perfectly that this matter is confidential. I have not even mentioned it to the members of my committee. I thought it my duty to consult you, and that's what I'm doing."

Fife's gaze at him showed no sign of melting into fondness. "You got a letter."

Shattuck nodded. "I did. An anonymous unsigned type-written letter. It may be from a crackpot, it probably is, but I didn't think it wise to ignore it."

"May I see it?"

"I have it," Colonel Ryder put in. He took a sheet of paper from under a weight on his desk and stepped across to pass it to his superior. But Fife was using his hands to pat the pockets of his jacket.

"Left my glasses upstairs. Read it."

Ryder did so.

"Dear sir: I address this to you because I understand that your investigating committee is authorized to inquire into matters of this sort. As

you know, in the emergency of the war the Army is being entrusted with the secrets of various industrial processes. This practice is probably justified in the circumstances, but it is being criminally abused. Some of the secrets, without patent or copyright protection, are being betrayed to those who intend to engage in post-war competition of the industries involved. Values amounting to tens of millions of dollars are being stolen from their rightful owners.

"Proof will be hard to get because of the difficulty of showing intent to defraud until it is put into practice after the war. I give you no details, but an honest and rigorous investigation will certainly disclose them. And I suggest a starting point: the death of Captain Albert Cross of Military Intelligence. He is supposed to have jumped, or fallen by accident, from the twelfth floor of the Bascombe Hotel in New York day before yesterday. Did he? What sort of inquiry had he been assigned to by his superior officers? What had he found out? You might start there.

"A Citizen"

Silence. Dead silence.

Colonel Tinkham cleared his throat. "Well-written letter," he observed, in the tone of a teacher commending a pupil for a good composition.

"May I look at it?" Nero Wolfe inquired.

Ryder handed it to him, and I got up and crossed the room to take a squint over Wolfe's shoulder. Tinkham and Lawson got the same notion and did likewise. Wolfe considerately held it at an angle so we could all see. It was a plain sheet of ordinary bond paper, and the text was single-spaced neatly in the center of the sheet with no errors or exings. From habit and experience I noted two mechanical peculiarities: the *c* hit below the line; and the *a* was off to the left—in *war*, for instance, it touched the top corner of the *w*. I was going on from there when Tinkham and Lawson finished and moved away, and Wolfe handed the sheet to me to return to Ryder.

"Hot stuff," Lawson said, sitting down. "He could a tale unfold, but he doesn't. Nothing but insinuations."

Fife asked him sarcastically, "Does that close the matter, Lieutenant?"

"Sir?"

"I ask, is your verdict final, or are we to be permitted to proceed?"

"Oh." Lawson showed color. "I beg your pardon, sir. I was merely observing—"

"There's another way to observe. Look and listen."

"Yes, sir."

"If I may be allowed—" Colonel Tinkham offered.

"Well?"

"Interesting points about that letter. It was written by a person who is incisive and highly literate and who also types expertly. Or it was dictated to a stenographer, which doesn't seem likely. The margining at the right is remarkably even. And the double spaces after periods—"

Wolfe made a noise, and Fife glanced at him. "What?"

"Nothing," Wolfe said. "I suppose I wouldn't mind if this chair were properly constructed and of a proper size. I suggest, if the discussion is to be at kindergarten level, that we all sit on the floor."

"Not a bad idea. We may come to that." Fife turned to Shattuck. "When did you get the letter?"

"In the mail Saturday morning," Shattuck told him. "Plain envelope of course, address typed, marked personal. Postmarked New York, Station R, 7:30 p.m. Friday. My first impulse was to turn it over to the F.B.I., but I decided that wouldn't be fair to you fellows, so I telephoned Harold—Colonel Ryder. I was coming to New York today anyway—speaking at a dinner tonight of the National Industrial Association—and we agreed this was the way to handle it."

"You haven't—you didn't take it up with General Carpenter?"

"No." Shattuck smiled. "After that performance when he appeared to testify before my committee a couple of months ago—I didn't feel like crossing his path."

"This is his path."

"I know, but he's not patrolling this sector of it at this moment—" Shattuck's eyes widened—"or is he?"

Fife shook his head. "He's stewing in Washington. Or sizzling. Or both. So you're turning the letter over to us for investigation. Is that it?"

"I don't know." Shattuck hesitated. He was meeting the general's eyes. "It came to me as chairman of a Congressional committee. I came here—to discuss the matter."

"You know—" Fife also hesitated. He went on, choosing words: "You know, of course, I could merely say military security is involved and the question cannot be discussed."

"I know," Shattuck agreed. "You could say that." He bore down a little on the "could."

Fife regarded him without affection.

"This is unofficial and off the record. There is nothing in that letter to show that the writer has any useful information. Anyone with any sense would know that in our war production, with thousands of men in positions of trust, and enormous interests and billions of dollars involved, things happen. Lots of them, probably including the sort of thing that letter hints at. One of the jobs of Military Intelligence is to help to prevent such things from happening, as far as we can."

"Of course," Shattuck put in, "I had no idea this would be a bolt from the blue for you."

"Thank you." Fife didn't sound grateful. "It isn't. Did you see that pink thing Ryder put in his desk drawer? You did. That's a new kind of grenade—not only new in construction, but in its contents. Somebody wanted some samples, and got them. Not the enemy—at least we don't think so. Captain Cross, who died last week, was working on it. Nobody on earth except the men in this room knew what Cross was doing. Cross found the trail, we don't know how, because he hadn't reported in since Monday, and now we may never know. Major Goodwin did a neat piece of work with an entry in Cross's memo book which apparently didn't mean anything, and found the grenades in a shipping carton in the checkroom at a bus terminal where Cross had left them. I tell you about this because Cross is mentioned in that letter, and also as an instance to show that if the writer of the letter wants to tell us anything we don't know he'll have to come again."

Shattuck remonstrated. "Good heavens, General, I know very well you weren't born yesterday. And ordinarily any anonymous letter I receive gets tossed in the wastebasket. But I thought you ought to know about it—and then the one specific thing in it—about Cross. Of course that was investigated?"

"It was. By the police."

"And," Shattuck insisted, "by you?" Then he added

hastily, "I think that's a proper question. Unofficially. Since a police investigation would be somewhat ineffectual unless they were told exactly what Cross was doing and were given the names of those who were—well—aware of it. I don't suppose you felt free to disclose that to the police?"

Fife said slowly, choosing his words again, "We co-operate with the police to the limit of discretion. As for your first question, proper or not, it is no military secret that Nero Wolfe has worked with us on various matters as a civilian consultant—since it has been published in newspapers. Do you regard Wolfe as a competent investigator?"

Shattuck smiled. "I'm a politician. You're not apt to find me in a minority of one."

"Well, he's investigating Cross's death. For us. If you find out who wrote you that letter, tell him that. That ought to satisfy him."

"It satisfies me," Shattuck declared. "I wonder if you'd mind—could I ask Mr. Wolfe a couple of questions?"

"Certainly. If he wants to answer them. I can't order him to. He's not in the Army."

Wolfe grunted. He was displaying all the signs, long familiar to me, of impatience, annoyance, discomfort, and an intense desire to get back home where chairs had been built to specifications to fit the case, and the beer was cold. He snapped:

"Mr. Shattuck. Perhaps I can make your questions unnecessary. Whether they come from idle curiosity, or are in fact sparks from the flame of your burning patriotism, Captain Cross was murdered. Does that answer them?"

Silence. Nobody made a sound. The look that General Fife flashed at Colonel Ryder met one coming back at him, and they both held. Colonel Tinkham's finger tip made contact with his mustache. Lieutenant Lawson stared at Wolfe, frowning. Shattuck's eyes, narrowed with a gleam in them, went from face to face.

Lieutenant Lawson said, "Oh, lord."

Chapter 2

Wolfe was pretending that nothing startling was happening. Not that any of the others could tell there was any pretense about it; nobody else knew him as I did. They probably were not even aware that his half-closed eyes were not missing the slightest twitch of a muscle among the group.

"I'm afraid," he said dryly, "that there's nothing in it for you, Mr. Shattuck. No votes, no acclaim, no applause from the multitude. I made the announcement in your presence because there's no way of proving it and probably never will be. Not a scrap of evidence. Anyone could have taken the hotel elevator and gone to Captain Cross's room on the twelfth floor, but no one was seen doing so. The mountain of the police machinery has labored—and no mouse. The window was wide open, and he was below on the pavement, squashed, dead. That's all."

"Then why the devil," Lawson demanded, "do you say he was murdered?"

"Because he was. He was as likely to fall from that window by accident as I would be to run for Congress—by accident. He did not deliberately jump out or crawl out. He phoned Colonel Ryder at eight o'clock that evening that he would come to the office in the morning to make a report; that he had had no sleep for two nights and had to rest. He sent a telegram to his fiancée in Boston that he would see her on Saturday. And then committed suicide? Pfui."

"Oh," Fife said, crossing his arms on the back of the chair again. "I thought—perhaps you had something."

"I have that." Wolfe wiggled a finger at him. "The man was murdered. But no guiding thread can be fastened to the smashed body on the pavement or in the room it fell from. The police have done a thorough job, and there is nothing. Some other point of departure is needed. If the motive was personal, out of his past as a man, the police may find it. They're trying to. If it was professional, out of his work as a soldier, we may find it in the course of our present activities. That is, if we are to continue? Along the line as it is being developed? With the same personnel?"

Fife studied the corner of Ryder's desk.

Wolfe said brusquely, "I put a question, General."

Fife's head jerked to him. "By all means. Continue? Certainly."

Shattuck said in a tone of satisfaction, "I don't think I need to ask you any questions, Mr. Wolfe."

"May I" Tinkham inquired, "offer a comment?"

"Go ahead," Fife told him.

"About the—personnel, as Mr. Wolfe put it. This is a complicated and difficult business; we all know that, even if it's all we know. And judging from what happened to Cross, if Mr. Wolfe is correct, somewhat dangerous. It's not the sort of enterprise to be entrusted to a kindergarten, and if that's Mr. Wolfe's opinion of us—specifically of me—"

"Skin tender?" Fife demanded. "The orders come from me."

"I was trying," Wolfe declared, "to educate you, Colonel, not obliterate you."

"I'm not worrying about my skin." Tinkham's voice had emotion in it, which for him was remarkable. "I would like to stay on this job. I merely want to be sure I understand the purpose of Mr. Wolfe's question about personnel."

"To get an answer." Wolfe was eyeing him. "I got it."

"All the same," Lawson broke in, addressing General Fife, "Colonel Tinkham has a point. For example, sir, you said just now the orders come from you. But they don't. At least they haven't in the two weeks I've been in on this. They come either from Colonel Ryder or from Nero Wolfe, and that's apt to be confusing, and besides, from the tone Wolfe takes he ought to have four stars on his shoulder, and he hasn't."

"My God," Fife said in disgust. "You too. Feelings hurt by the tone Wolfe takes! He's right. This damn Army is turning into a kindergarten. And if I ship you overseas or back to Washington I'll only get somebody worse." He turned to Wolfe. "What about you and Ryder? Has there been any conflict in orders?"

"None that I know of," Wolfe said patiently.

Fife switched to Ryder. "Any that you know of?"

"No, sir." Ryder's answer was a brush-off, as if the matter were of no interest or significance. "Mr. Wolfe has been entirely co-operative and helpful. No one but a fool would resent his mannerisms. But I ought to say— The circumstances— You should know that there will be a change in the setup. I would like to make a request. I respectfully request permission to go to Washington to see General Carpenter. Today."

For the third time a sudden dead silence fell. Since the rest of us were not professional soldiers, we didn't grasp immediately all the implications of that request made in that manner; what got us was what happened to General Fife's face. It froze. I had never seen the old bozo look stupid before, but he sure did then, staring across Ryder's desk at him.

"Perhaps, sir," Ryder said, meeting the stare, "I should add that it is not a personal matter. I wish to see General Carpenter on Army business. I have a reservation on the five o'clock plane."

Silence again. The muscles of Fife's neck moved, then he spoke. "This is a strange performance, Colonel." His voice was cold and controlled. "I suppose it can be charged to your unfamiliarity with Army custom. This sort of thing is usually done, if at all, in a less public manner. I offer a suggestion, not official. If you care to, you may discuss it with me privately. Now. Or after lunch, when you've thought it over."

"I'm sorry." Ryder didn't sound happy, but he sounded firm. "It wouldn't help any. I know what I'm doing, sir."

"By God, I hope you do."

"Yes, sir. I do. Have I permission to go?"

"You have." The expression on Fife's face plainly added, and keep right on going and never come back, but he was being an officer and gentleman in the presence of witnesses. To be fair to him, he didn't do a bad job at all. He stood up and told Tinkham and Lawson they could go, which they did. Then he invited John Bell Shattuck to have lunch with him, and Shattuck accepted. Fife turned to Wolfe and said it would be a pleasure to have him join them, but Wolfe declined with thanks, saying he had another engagement, which was a lie. He disliked all restaurants, and claimed that the one where General Fife lunched put sulphur in curried lamb. Fife and Shattuck went out together, without another word to Ryder.

Wolfe stood by Ryder's desk, frowning down at him, waiting for him to look up. Finally Ryder did.

"I think," Wolfe said, "that you're a nincompoop. Not a conclusion, merely an opinion."

"File it for reference," Ryder said.

"I shall do so. Your brain is not functioning. Your son died. Captain Cross, one of your men, was killed. You are in no condition to make hard decisions. If you have an intelligent friend with a head that works, consult him. Or even a lawyer. Or me."

"You?" Ryder said. "Now that would be good. That would be just fine."

Wolfe lifted his shoulders a quarter of an inch, let them drop back into place, said, "Come, Archie," and started for the door. I returned the suitcase to the chair where I had found it, and followed him. Sergeant Bruce glanced up as we passed through the anteroom. Wolfe ignored her. I halted at her desk and said, "I've got something in my eye."

"That's too bad," she said and stood up. "Which eye? Let me see." I thought, *Good lord, where's she been all these years, falling for that old gag?* I bent over to stare into her eyes, not ten inches away, and she stared back into mine.

"I see it," she said.

"Yeah? What is it?"

"It's me. In both eyes. No way of getting it out."

She sat down again and went on typing, absolutely deadpan. I had utterly misjudged her. "Okay," I conceded, "you're one up," and dashed after Wolfe, and found him at the elevator.

There were about a dozen assorted questions I had in mind to ask him, with a chance of finding him inclined to supply at least some of the answers, but the opportunity never arrived. Of course en route was no good, with him in the back seat resenting. The minute we got home he beat it to the kitchen to give Fritz a hand with lunch. They were trying out some kind of a theory involving chicken fat and eggplant. At the table business was always taboo, so I had to listen to him explain why sustained chess-playing would ruin any good field general. Then, because he had missed his morning session up in the plant rooms with the orchids, he had to go up there, and I knew that was no place to start a conversation. I asked him if I should report back downtown, and he said no, he might need me, and since my orders were to nurse Nero Wolfe as required, I went into the office, on the ground floor, did some chores at my desk, and listened to news broadcasts.

At 3:25 the phone rang. It was General Fife. He instructed me, speaking to a subordinate, to deliver Nero Wolfe at his office at four o'clock. I informed him it wouldn't work. He stated that I should make it work and rang off.

I called him back and said, "Listen. Sir. Do you want him or don't you? I respectfully remind you that there is no way on God's earth of getting him except for you, or at least a colonel, to speak to him and tell him what you want."

"Damn him. Let me talk to him."

I buzzed the plant room extension, got Wolfe, was told by him to listen in, and did so. It was nothing new. All Fife would say on the phone was that he must have a talk with Wolfe, together with Tinkham and Lawson and me, without delay. Wolfe finally said he'd go. When he came downstairs ten minutes later, I told him, on the way out to the car, "One item you may want, in case you've got it entered that it was something that was said this morning that made Ryder decide to go to Washington to see Carpenter. He already had his suitcase there packed."

"I saw it. Confound the blasted Germans. Don't let it give that jerk when you start. I'm in no humor for pleasantries."

We were in the lobby at 17 Duncan Street at 3:55, a few minutes ahead of time. Absent-mindedly, from force of habit, I said "ten" to the elevator man, and it wasn't until after we had got out at the tenth that I woke up. Fife's office was on the eleventh. Wolfe was starting the usual rigmarole with the corporal. I said, "Hey, our mistake. We're on the—"

I never finished, because it came at that instant. The noise wasn't loud, certainly it wasn't deafening, but there was something about it that hit you in the spine. Or maybe it wasn't the noise, but the shaking of the building. Everybody agreed later that the building shook. I doubt it. Maybe it was something that happened to the air. Anyhow, for a second everything inside of me stopped working, and, judging from the look on the corporal's face, him ditto. Then we both stared in all directions. But Wolfe had already started for the door leading to the inner corridor, barking at me, "It's that thing. Didn't I tell you?"

I beat him to the door with a skip and a jump, and closed it when we were through. In the corridor people, mostly in uniform, were looking out of doors, and popping out. Some were headed for the far end of the corridor, a couple of them running. Voices came from up ahead, and a curtain of smoke or dust, or both, came drifting toward us, pushing a sour sharp smell in front of it. We went on into it, to the end, and turned right.

It was one swell mess. It looked exactly like a

blurred radiophoto with the caption, *Our Troops Taking an Enemy Machine-Gun Nest in a Sicilian Village.* Debris, crumbled plaster, a door hanging by one hinge, most of a wall gone, men in uniform looking grim. Standing in what had been the doorway, facing out, was Colonel Tinkham. When two men tried to push past him into what had been Ryder's room, he barred the way and bellowed, "Stand back! Back to that corner!" They backed up, but only about five paces, where they bumped into Wolfe and me. Others were behind us and around us.

From the commotion in the rear one voice was suddenly heard above the others: "General Fife!"

A lane opened up, and in a moment Fife came striding through. At sight of him Tinkham moved forward from the doorway, and behind Tinkham, from within, came Lieutenant Lawson. They both saluted, which may sound silly, but somehow didn't look silly. Fife returned it and asked, "What's in there?"

Lawson spoke. "Colonel Ryder, sir."

"Dead?"

"Good God, yes. All blown apart."

"Anyone else hurt?"

"No, sir. No sign of anybody."

"I'll take a look. Tinkham, clear this hall. Everybody back where they belong. No one is to leave the premises."

Nero Wolfe rumbled in my ear, "This confounded dust. And smell. Come, Archie."

That was the only occasion I remember when he willingly climbed a flight of stairs. Not knowing what orders had already been given to the corporal by the elevators, he probably wanted to avoid delay. Nobody interfered with us, since going to the eleventh floor was not leaving the premises. He marched straight through the anteroom to General Fife's office, with me at his heels, straight to the big leather chair with its back to a window, sat down, got himself properly adjusted, and told me:

"Telephone that place, wherever it is, and tell them to send some beer."

Chapter 3

Our old friend and foe, Inspector Cramer of the Homicide Squad, tilted his cigar up from the corner of his mouth and again ran his eye over the sheet of paper in his hand. I had typed the thing myself from General Fife's dictation. It read:

> Colonel Harold Ryder of the United States Army was accidentally killed at four o'clock this afternoon when a grenade exploded in his office at 17 Duncan Street. It is not known exactly how the accident occurred. The grenade was of a new type, with great explosive power, not yet issued to our forces, and was in Colonel Ryder's possession officially, in the line of duty. Colonel Ryder was attached to the New York unit of Military Intelligence headed by Brigadier General Mortimer Fife.

"Even so," Cramer growled, "it's pretty skimpy."

Wolfe was still in the big leather chair, with three empty beer bottles on the window sill behind him. Fife was seated behind his desk. I had stepped across to hand Cramer the paper and then propped myself against the wall at ease.

"You may elaborate it as you see fit," Fife suggested without enthusiasm. He looked a little bedraggled.

"Sure." Cramer removed his cigar. "Elaborate it with what?" He waved it away with the cigar. "You're an Army man. I'm a policeman. I'm paid by the City of New York to investigate sudden or suspicious death. So I need facts. Such as, where did the grenade come from and how did it get into his desk drawer? How much carelessness would it take to make it go off accidentally? Such as, can I see one like it? Military security says nothing doing. What I don't know won't hurt me. But it does hurt me."

Fife said, "I let you bring your men in and go over it."

"Damn sweet of you." Cramer was really upset. "This building is not United States property and it's in my borough, and you talk about letting me!" He waggled the sheet of paper. "Look here, General. You know how it is as well as I do. Ordinarily, if there was no background to this, I'd rub it out without a murmur. But Captain Cross was working under Ryder, that's one fact I've got, and Cross was murdered. And right here in the building, here when it happened, and sitting here now in your office when I enter, is Nero Wolfe. I've known Wolfe for something like twenty years, and I'll tell you this. Show me a corpse, any corpse, under the most ideal and innocent circumstances, with a certificate signed by every doctor in New York, including the Medical Examiner. Then show me Nero Wolfe anywhere within reach, exhibiting the faintest sign of interest, and I order the squad to go to work immediately."

"Bosh." Wolfe nearly opened his eyes. "Have I ever imposed on you, Mr. Cramer?"

"What!" Cramer goggled at him. "You've never done anything else!"

"Nonsense. At any rate, I'm not imposing on you now. All this is a waste of time. You know very well you can't bulldoze the Army, especially not this branch of it." Wolfe sighed. "I'll do you a favor. I believe the mess down there hasn't been disturbed. I'll go down and take a look at it. I'll consider the situation, what I know of it, which is more than you're likely ever to find out. Tomorrow I'll phone you and give you my opinion. How will that do?"

"And meanwhile?" Cramer demanded.

"Meanwhile you take your men out of here and stay out. I remind you of the opinion I gave you regarding Captain Cross."

Cramer stuck his cigar back in his mouth and clamped his teeth on it, folded the paper and put it in his pocket, leaned back, and hooked his thumbs in the armholes of his vest, with an air implying that he was there for the duration. He was glaring at Wolfe. Then he jerked forward in his chair and growled, "Phone me tonight."

"No." Wolfe was positive. "Tomorrow."

Cramer regarded him three seconds more, then stood up and addressed General Fife. "I've got nothing against the Army. As an Army. We can't fight a war without an Army. But it would suit me fine if the whole goddamn outfit would clear out of my borough and get on ships bound for Germany." He turned and went.

Wolfe sighed again.

Fife pursed his lips and shook his head. "You can't blame him."

"No," Wolfe agreed. "Mr. Cramer is constantly

leaping at the throat of evil and finding himself holding on for dear life to the tip of its tail."

"What?" Fife squinted at him. "Oh. I suppose so." He got out his handkerchief and used it on his brow and face and neck, removing an old smear but producing new ones. He shot me a glance, and went back to Wolfe. "About Ryder. I'd rather discuss it with you privately."

Wolfe shook his head. "Not without Major Goodwin. I use his memory. Also for years I've found his presence an irritant which stimulates my cells. What about Ryder? Wasn't it an accident?"

"I suppose it was. What do you think?"

"I haven't thought. Nowhere to start. Could it have been an accident? If he took it from the drawer and it dropped on the floor?"

"No," Fife declared. "Out of the question. Anyway, it was somewhere above the desk when it exploded. The desk top was smashed downward. And that pin is joltproof. It requires a sharp firm lateral pull."

"Then it wasn't an accident," Wolfe said placidly. "Suicide remains, and so does— By the way, what about that woman in his anteroom? That female in uniform. Where was she?"

"Not there. Out to lunch."

"Indeed." Wolfe's brows went up. "At four o'clock?"

"So she told Tinkham. He spoke with her when she returned. She's waiting outside now. I sent for her."

"Get her in here. And may I—?"

"Certainly." Fife lifted his phone and spoke in it.

In a moment the door opened and Sergeant Bruce entered. She came in three steps, getting the three of us at a glance, stopped with her heels together, and snapped a salute. She appeared to be quite herself, only extremely solemn. She advanced when she was told to.

"This is Nero Wolfe," Fife said. "He'll ask you some questions, and you'll answer as from me."

"Yes, sir."

"Sit down," Wolfe told her. "Archie, if you'll move that chair around? Excuse me, General, if I violate regulations, a major waiting on a sergeant, but I find it impossible to regard a woman as a soldier and don't intend to try." He looked at her. "Miss Bruce. That's your name?"

"Yes, sir. Dorothy Bruce."

"You were at lunch when that thing exploded?"

"Yes, sir." Her voice was as clear and composed as it had been when she told me she was in my eye.

"Is that your usual lunch hour? Four o'clock?"

"No, sir. Shall I explain?"

"Please. With a minimum of *sirs*. I am not a field marshal in disguise. Go ahead."

"Yes, sir. I beg your pardon, that was automatic. I have no usual lunch hour. At Colonel Ryder's request, I mean his order, I have been going to lunch whenever he did, so I would be on duty when he was in his office. Today he didn't go to lunch—that is, I don't think he did—at least he didn't come out through the anteroom and let me know he was going, as he always had done. When he called me in at a quarter to four to give me some instructions, he asked if I had had lunch and said he had forgotten about it, and told me to go then. I went down to the corner drugstore and had a sandwich and coffee. I got back at twenty past four."

Wolfe's half-closed eyes never left her face. "The corner drugstore?" he inquired mildly. "Didn't you hear the explosion or see any excitement?"

"No, sir. The drugstore is a block and a half away, around on Mitchell Street."

"You say Colonel Ryder didn't go to lunch? Was he

constantly in his office right through to a quarter to four?"

"I think I qualified that. I said he didn't come out through the anteroom. Of course he could have left by the other door at any time, the one direct from his room to the outer hall, and re-entered the same way. He often used that door."

"Was that door kept locked?"

"Usually it was, yes, sir." She hesitated. "Should I confine myself to the question?"

"We want information, Miss Bruce. If you have it we want it."

"Only about that door. Colonel Ryder had a key to it, of course. But on two occasions I saw him, going out that way, intending to return soon, push the button that released the lock so that he could get back in without using the key. If you want details like that—"

"We do. Have you got some more?"

She shook her head. "No, sir. I only mentioned that because you asked if that door was kept locked."

"Have you any idea how this thing happened?"

"Why—" Her eyes flickered. "I thought—I understand it was a grenade Colonel Ryder had in his desk."

Fife shot at her, "How do you know it was a grenade?"

Her head pivoted to him. "Because, sir, everyone is saying that it was. If it was a secret—it isn't now."

"Of course it isn't," Wolfe said peevishly. "If you please, General. Have you any idea, Miss Bruce, how the grenade got exploded?"

"Certainly not! I mean—no, sir."

"It is permissible to mean certainly not," Wolfe murmured at her. "You know nothing whatever about it?"

"No, sir."

"What were the instructions Colonel Ryder gave you at a quarter to four when he called you in?"

"Only routine matters. He said he was leaving for the day, and told me to sign the letters, and that he wouldn't be in tomorrow and I should cancel any appointments he had."

"That was all?"

"Yes, sir."

"You were his confidential secretary?"

"Well—I don't know how confidential I was. I have been here less than two weeks and had never met Colonel Ryder before. I suppose, really, for that sort of job, I was still on trial. I only came up from Washington ten days ago."

"What had you been doing in Washington?"

"I was secretary to one of General Carpenter's assistants. Lieutenant Colonel Adams."

Wolfe grunted, and closed his eyes. Sergeant Bruce sat and waited. Fife had his lips pressed into a straighter line than usual, apparently restraining himself. He wasn't accustomed to playing audience while someone else asked questions, but probably hadn't forgotten the time Wolfe had made him look silly in front of three lieutenants and a private who had been tailing a distinguished visitor from Mexico. Wolfe grunted again, this time what I called his number-three grunt, which meant he was displeased, and I had no idea what had riled him. I thought Sergeant Bruce had been courteous, co-operative, and cute. Then he opened his eyes, shifted his center of gravity, and got his hands braced on the chair arms, and of course that explained it. He was displeased because he had decided he was going to stand up.

He did so, rumbling, "That's all for the present, Miss Bruce. You'll be available, of course. As you know,

General, I promised Mr. Cramer I'd take a look at the ruins. Come, Archie." He took a step. But Fife stopped him:

"Just a minute, please. All right, Bruce, you may go."

She arose, hesitated a moment, then faced the general. "May I ask you something, sir?"

"Yes. What?"

"They won't let me take anything from my room, sir. I have some things—just personal belongings—I was away over the week-end and came direct to the office from the station this morning. Colonel Ryder gave me a passout—but I suppose it isn't valid—now."

"All right, go ahead." Fife sounded fed up. "I'll send instructions to Colonel Tinkham— By the way—" He squinted at her. "You have no office and no job. Temporarily. You sound intelligent and capable. Are you?"

"Yes, sir."

"The devil you are. We'll see. Report in my anteroom tomorrow morning. If you have favorite tools, bring them with you. You'd better get them out of there now, that place will be cleaned up tonight. Tell Colonel Tinkham—no, I'll tell him. You may go."

She saluted, whirled, and went out like a soldier.

Fife waited until the door had closed behind her before he spoke to Wolfe. "You were saying something. Before we had Bruce come in."

"Nothing of importance." Wolfe was curt, as always when he talked standing up. "Accident, no. Suicide, possibly. Murder? It appears that anyone might have entered that room when Ryder wasn't there, without being observed, since Ryder might have gone out by the hall door and left it unlocked."

"Entered? And then what?"

"Oh, as his fancy struck him. Got the grenade from

the desk. Took it away. Later, when Miss Bruce left, entered the anteroom, opened the door there into Ryder's room, pulled the pin from the grenade, tossed it at Ryder, and pumped back into the hall. That, of course, raises the interesting point that presumably only six people knew the grenade was there: Tinkham, Lawson, Shattuck, you, Goodwin, me. I know of nothing that eliminates anyone but the last two. Take you, for instance. You've been here all afternoon?"

Fife's lips tightened in a grim smile. "That's a good plan; start at the top. Yes, I've been here, but I'm afraid I can't prove I haven't left this room. Shattuck came back with me after lunch, but he left around two-thirty. Then I dictated for half an hour, but after that I guess you have me."

Wolfe grunted. "Bah! This is nothing but gibberish, as it stands now. I'll run down and take a look."

He stalked out and I followed. As I was pulling the front door to, softly since it was a general's door, I heard Fife at his phone asking for Colonel Tinkham.

There was delay down on the tenth floor, at the scene. In what had been the doorway to Colonel Ryder's room from the hall stood a corporal with accouterments. The fact that he would have weighed over 200 even without the accouterments made it seem all the more formidable when he said no one could enter, including us. When Wolfe told me to go and get Fife and haul him down there, I stalled; and, as I expected, in a minute Colonel Tinkham arrived to tell the corporal it was okay, orders from General Fife. Then Tinkham joined our party by preceding us into the shambles. Wolfe asked him if anything had been taken out, and Tinkham said no, the police had given it a good going over but hadn't been permitted to remove anything, and neither had anyone else.

It was still broad daylight in that corner room, with a nice breeze from the windows, since there was no glass left in them. As we looked things over, stepping to avoid chunks of plaster and similar obstructions, various details were worthy of note. By a freak of the blast, the partition to the hall was a wreck, but the one to the anteroom only had a couple of cracks. The door to the anteroom was standing open, and looked intact but a little cockeyed. Two of the chairs were nothing but splinters, four were battered and scarred, and Ryder's own chair, against the wall back of his desk, didn't have a mark. The desk top was smashed and pockmarked, as if someone had first dropped a two-ton weight on it and then used it for a target with a shotgun loaded with slugs. On it and all around that area were bloodstains, from single drops up to a big blob the size of a dishpan on the floor back of the desk. The remains of the suitcase and its contents, also on the floor, were over near the door to the anteroom, the contents strewn around, the suitcase twisted and riddled so that for a second I didn't recognize it. Everywhere, in all directions, were little pieces of metal, as small as the head of a pin or as big as a thumbnail, black on one side and pink on the other. Anyone anywhere in that room when the thing exploded would have stopped at least a dozen of them— and they would have stopped him. I dropped a couple in my pocket to add to my collection in a drawer at home.

I also acquired another souvenir. A piece of folded paper in the jumble of the contents of the suitcase looked familiar. Wolfe and Tinkham were at the other side of the room. I stooped and snared the paper, saw at a glance that it was the anonymous letter to Shattuck that had started the morning's conference, and slipped it into my inside breast pocket.

We were still poking around, observing and commenting, and Tinkham was still acting as chaperon, when I became aware that company had arrived next door. I stepped through to the anteroom. Sergeant Bruce was standing there, frowning at a tennis racket she held in her hand.

"Damaged?" I inquired brightly.

"No, sir."

Nuts, I thought, *this sir stuff is worse than a suit of armor*. She put the racket into a fiber shipping carton that stood on the floor with its end flaps open, and moved around behind her desk. The place was thick with dust, and things were displaced, but nothing seemed to be hurt much.

"Can I help?"

"No, sir, thanks."

Some day, I said to myself grimly, or rather to her but not audibly, *matters will be so arranged that, whether you're worth it or not, sir will be as far from your mind as—*

"Archie!" It was a bellow.

"At ease," I told her gruffly, and faded.

Wolfe and Tinkham were at the other end of the room, over by the corporal.

"Take me home," Wolfe said.

There was never any dillydallying when Wolfe had decided to go home. The look on Tinkham's face gave me the impression that he either had some questions he would like to ask, or that he had got no answers to some he had already asked, but all he did get was a request from Wolfe to inform General Fife that he would communicate with him in the morning.

There was a crowd down on the sidewalk, and a bigger one across the street. Any broken glass that had descended from the tenth floor two hours ago had been cleaned up. As we made our way through to where the car was parked, I heard a man tell a girl, "A big bomb exploded and killed eighty people and two generals." That was a little surprising, but driving home, going up Varick Street, Wolfe said something that was much more so. From the back seat he told me plainly, "Go a little faster, Archie." That flammed me. As I said, he never talked while undergoing the hazards of motorized movement, and him asking for more speed was about the same as a private asking for more K.P. Anyhow, I obliged.

He muttered under his breath, probably a prayer of thanks, as we stopped in front of the house, and then, as I opened my door and started to wriggle from behind the wheel, he spoke. "Don't get out. You're going somewhere."

"Oh. I am."

"Yes. Back downtown. General Fife said that place will be cleaned up tonight. They may start at any moment, and I want that suitcase. Get it and bring it here. Just the case. I don't want the contents. Exactly as it is; don't bend it or do any tampering with it."

I had twisted around to glare at him. He had opened his door and was climbing out. "You mean," I demanded, "Ryder's suitcase?"

"I do." He was on the sidewalk. "It's important. Also it is doubly important that no one should see you taking it. Especially Lieutenant Lawson, Colonel Tinkham, General Fife, or Miss Bruce, but preferably no one."

I seldom sputter, but I sputtered. "That suitcase—from under their noses—listen. Will you settle for the moon? Glad to get the moon for you. Do you realize—"

"Certainly I realize. It's a difficult errand. I doubt if there is another man anywhere, in the Army or out, who could safely be entrusted with it."

He sure wanted that suitcase, to be ladling it out like that.

"Bushwah," I said, and opened my door and crawled out, and headed for the stoop.

He snapped after me. "Where are you going?"

"To get a receptacle!" I called over my shoulder. "Do you think I'm going to hang it around my neck?"

Three minutes later I was on my way back to Duncan Street, the rear seat occupied not by Wolfe but by a man-size suitcase that I had got from the closet in his room. I had one of my own just as big, but I wasn't going to risk my personal property in addition to my career as a warrior. I was sorry I hadn't read up more fully on the regulations about courts-martial. Not that I wasted the minutes en route being sorry. I used them to consider ways and means. My watch said 6:30, and at that hour of the day I couldn't tell what I would be up against until I had executed a patrol. You never knew around there; anyone might be out or in; anyone might leave for the day any time between four and midnight. I had my mind started on about three and a half different plans, but by the time I got to Duncan Street I had decided that I couldn't lay out a campaign until I had looked the ground over and done a reconnaissance on the enemy.

On the tenth floor I returned the corporal's salute, indicating by my posture that the receptable, in my left hand, was a little hefty, assumed an urgent expression, and asked him if he had seen Lieutenant Lawson go out.

"Yes, sir. He left about twenty minutes ago."

"Damn it. Colonel Tinkham too?"

"No, sir. I think he's in his office."

"Have you seen General Fife around?"

"Not for an hour or more, sir. He may be upstairs."

I breezed through to the inner corridor. No one in sight. The door to my room was about twenty paces down normally, and it took me not more than fourteen. Inside I took a breath, and deposited the big suitcase on my desk. It began to seem more possible. Like this. I go to the scene and tell the corporal Nero Wolfe sent me back to do a close-up on something. I enter and examine the top of Ryder's desk with my little glass. I make noises of dissatisfaction and tell the corporal to go ask Major Goodman if I may borrow his big magnifying glass, Goodman's office being on the eleventh floor. The corporal goes, I grab the suitcase, dive down the hall to my room, and cache it in Wolfe's case. That would be the only risk, the five seconds negotiating the hall. The rest would be pie. I turned it over and around, looking for a way to reduce the risk still more, but decided that was the minimum.

I got the little glass from a drawer of my desk and stuck it in my pocket, went out and down the corridor, turned the corner, saw that the same corporal was on guard and no one else around, said my little piece to him, was passed in without any question, crossed to Ryder's desk, and began inspecting it with the glass. But my heart wasn't in my work because I had had plenty of time, approaching the desk, to perceive that the suitcase wasn't there.

Chapter 4

I continued to inspect the desk, remarking to myself meanwhile, "Of all the blank blink blonk blunk luck."

Since nothing more helpful than that occurred to me, I finally straightened up for a comprehensive survey. As far as I could see, everything was as before with the single exception of the suitcase. I went over to the corporal.

"Anyone been in here since Colonel Tinkham and Wolfe and I left?"

"No, sir. Oh yes, Colonel Tinkham came back shortly afterward. General Fife was with him."

"Oh," I said casually, "then I guess they took that chair."

"Chair?"

"Yeah, one of the chairs Wolfe wanted me to examine—it seems to be gone—I'll go and see—"

"There can't be a chair gone, sir. Nobody took any chair or anything else."

"You're sure of that? Not even General Fife or Colonel Tinkham?"

"No, sir. Nobody."

I grinned at him. "If I was Nero Wolfe, corporal,

which I'm not, I would advise you to confine your assurances to the boundaries of your knowledge. That's his way of putting it. You say positively that nobody took anything. But I notice you stand here in the doorway facing the hall, your back to the room. There's no glass left in the windows. How do you know a paratrooper didn't come in that way and take anything he wanted?"

For half a second he looked slightly startled, and for the next half a second the look in his eyes plainly indicated what he would have said, and probably done, if we had been just people instead of a corporal and a major. All he did say was "Yes, sir."

"Okay," I told him as man to man. "Probably I counted wrong. Skip it. I always get mixed up when I go above six."

I went down the corridor to my room, sat on the edge of my desk, and applied logic. Of course it was obvious, if the corporal wasn't either blind or a liar. Mental operations like figuring the cube root of minus two I leave to Nero Wolfe, but I can do simple addition and subtraction. So I pulled the phone over and got Captain Foster, in charge of personnel, and asked him for the home address of Sergeant Dorothy Bruce.

He was inclined to be flippant, but I told him the request was official and he loosened up. The Bronx or Brooklyn would have been a blow, since I was taking the trip not on information or a hunch, but only on logic, and I was relieved when he gave me a number on West Eleventh Street. That was right on the way home. Toting the receptacle which apparently I had brought along just for the ride, I evacuated via the elevator, went to the car, and started back uptown.

The Eleventh Street number was the only modern structure in a block of old brownstones. Leaving the receptacle in the car, I entered and brushed past the hallman in a military stride, columned left on a guess, spied the elevator, and said brusquely to the girl loitering outside, "Bruce." Manifestly I was not a man to be questioned. She followed me in and started us up, stopped and opened the door at the seventh, and said musically, "Seven C." I found it, the second on the right down the hall, pushed the button, and after a little wait the door opened. But it swung only to a gap of a few inches, so as a precaution I unobtrusively planted a foot beyond the line of the sill.

"Oh!" she said in a tone of surprise. I didn't say pleased surprise. "Major Goodwin!"

"Right," I said cheerfully. "You sure have a memory for faces. My eye's bothering me again."

"That's too bad, sir." She seemed perfectly affable, but the door showed no inclination to exercise its hinges. "As I told you, I'm afraid there's nothing I can do about it."

"Not in this bum light you can't. Nice little place you've got here. Are these your own things, or do you rent it furnished? Some of them must be yours. It just looks like you."

"Oh, thank you, sir. It's the woman's touch, of course."

"Yeah. I never saw a more attractive door. I'll tell you what. I could say, Sergeant Bruce, I wish to come in and have a little talk with you. Or I could simply push and enter. Let's compromise. You propel the door and I'll propel me."

She nearly laughed, but it didn't get beyond a sort of a chuckle. Anyhow the door swung open and she invited me nicely, "Come in, Major." Also she closed it. The foyer was about the size of a suitcase. At a gesture I preceded her into a room which wasn't like her at all because it wasn't like anybody. Pure month-to-month-

or-reduction-on-a-lease. Two windows. A couch and three chairs. Door to kitchenette and door to bedroom. A glance gave me that, and when I turned she was there and smiling at me. It was absolutely a female smile, and at any previous moment I would have considered it a big step forward, but something had come between us if logic was worth its salt. Still I kept it on a friendly basis.

I asked her, "Remember that carton you were packing your things in at the office? I need one exactly that size, and if you're through with it I'd like to make an offer."

She was good. She was very good. The way the smile went and her lips parted a little and her eyes widened—it was just what you would expect if I had said something fairly silly and unquestionably cuckoo.

Then she smiled again and said, "I can get one for you wholesale."

I shook my head. "Your mistake. You didn't say *sir*. The idea is this. I won't be happy until I see that carton, and I'm hell-bent for happiness. Either you trot it out or I tour the place. You can save me trouble and both of us time."

"Is that an official command, sir? Are you here as my superior officer or as—yourself?"

"Any way you like it. Whichever you prefer. Take it going and coming and call it both, but get the carton."

She moved. To get to the door to the bedroom she had to detour around me, which she did, and disappeared through the opening. But I had decided that probably not much was beyond her up to sailing off on a broomstick, so I stepped across on my toes to the doorway to keep her in sight. But either I made some noise or she was suspicious by nature, because halfway across the bedroom she turned and saw me. She came back and took hold of the knob of the door, obviously intending to close it when the obstruction, namely me, was removed.

"You can wait out there," she said, and meant it. "I'll bring the carton."

I was not particularly enjoying things, and it was getting too prolonged for me. Evidently she had been headed for a closed closet door at the far corner of the room. I stepped past her, rounded the foot of the bed and got to the door, and pulled it open. I admit I was surprised enough to back up two steps when a uniform, erect in the closet, moved toward me, and there was Lieutenant Kenneth Lawson. He came out and stood and looked at me. He didn't salute.

"Indeed," I said. That was Nero Wolfe's word, and I never used it except in moments of stress, and it severely annoyed me when I caught myself using it, because when I look in a mirror I prefer to see me as is, with no skin grafted from anybody else's hide, even Nero Wolfe's.

Lawson, as I have said, was big and strong and handsome. The situation, as it stood, seemed to indicate that anything was possible, and I had no desire to join Cross and Ryder on the other side of the river, so I backed into the closet with the door opened as wide as it would go. It wasn't necessary to do any searching. The carton was right there, bound with cord. I yanked it out, jerked off the cord, lifted the flaps, and was looking at shredded pigskin. For logic, one hit, one run, no errors. I closed the flaps and got the cord back on. Among other things I didn't know, at that point, was whether Lawson was there on purely personal business or whether he was a partner in the enterprise of salvaging damaged luggage, so the position was delicate in more ways than one.

Lawson said, with no special sign of agitation, "I heard Bruce ask you—and it might clear things up a little—is this an official visit, Major?"

After all, he had me. Wolfe had told me to get the suitcase without the knowledge of Fife, and Fife was my commanding officer. My ignorance was stupendous. Was Lawson straight and would he report to Fife? Was Lawson a crook or a murderer, or both—and would he report to Fife anyway to cover up? Were Lawson and Sergeant Bruce— But there was no sense standing there all night asking myself questions I couldn't answer, with them staring at me.

I spoke. "Ladies and gentlemen. I have been assigned, as you know, to assist Nero Wolfe in work he is doing for the Army. I'm now going to report to him, and take this carton with me. Up to there, as far as you're concerned, since you're only a non-com and a shavetail, we can put it that the only difference between General Eisenhower and me is that he's not here. But beyond that we're just folks. If on my way out Lawson tries to trip me or hit me with a chair I won't appeal to authority, now or later. I'll merely knock his block off."

A corner of Lawson's mouth was turned up. "I wasn't going to be so crude," he said coldly, "but now I don't know."

"Make up your mind, brother," I told him, and focused on Sergeant Bruce. "So I offer a suggestion. Not an order from Major Goodwin, just a person-to-person call. How about accompanying the carton and me to Wolfe's place? I've got a car down in front. The trip might do you good."

If she had flashed a glance at Lawson that would have answered at least one of my questions, but all she did was cock her head at me.

"I think," she said, "that I ought to tell you you'll probably be sorry for this, Major."

"I already am. I don't like any part of it. Are you coming?"

"Certainly. That carton and its contents belong to me." She moved, crossing to Lawson and putting her hand on his arm. "Ken darling, this is nothing. Really. But I'm afraid—I don't know how long it will take. I'll phone you later. And perhaps you had better phone my sister in Washington—right away."

"I could," he growled, "wring him out and hang him up to dry."

"I'm sure you could." She patted his arm. "But you behave yourself. There's more than one way to—cure a cold. Phone me later, Ken?"

"I will."

"Be sure the door's locked when you leave. Are we going, Major?"

Lawson didn't move a muscle as I passed him, with the carton in the hand nearest him, so the other hand would be free in case he decided to show her how big and brave he was. But either she was the boss and he was obeying orders, or he wanted to be alone to think. I signified that she, being a lady, should go first, and she did so, stopping in the other room only to get her peck-measure cap from the table, and letting me close the door after us and push the button for the elevator as if she enjoyed having a male escort attend to such details.

On the street, I put the carton in the rear and her in the front, went around and slid in behind the wheel, beside her, and got going. No conversation. Apparently there wasn't going to be any. But as I waited for a light at Twenty-Third Street, suddenly she spoke.

"I wonder if you'd like to do me a little favor."

"I doubt it. What? Want me to phone your sister in Washington?"

She made a little noise, between a chuckle and a gurgle. Three hours earlier I would have thought it very attractive. "No," she said, "nothing as complicated as that. Just to stop a minute, anywhere there's a place at the curb, so I can ask you something."

The light changed and we rolled. A block farther on a roomy space came in view, and I steered into it and shut off the engine.

"Okay. Ask me something."

"I hope your eye feels better."

Her tone made it plain that it was not a sergeant speaking to a major. It abolished all consideration of worldly rank and superficial barriers. Not that it conveyed the impression that she intended to seduce me right there on Sixth Avenue in the midst of traffic, but it did indicate that a closer understanding between the two of us would be a natural and wholesome development.

I said, "It feels fine. That all?"

"No. I wish it was." She was turned to me full face, and I was reciprocating. "I wish there was nothing, I mean with you and me, except silly little pleasant things like that. Don't think I'm being obvious. I'm just clever enough, just barely, to know how clever you are. If I were a fool, I might think I could start your head whirling in no time, parked here on our way to Nero Wolfe, but I know better than to try idiotic tricks with you."

I grinned at her. "You do know how to handle your lips and eyes, though. And especially your voice. Which you were going to use to ask me something."

She nodded. "Tell me, does Nero Wolfe want that

carton just to see if I took something that doesn't belong to me?"

"No." I couldn't see that hedging was called for. "He doesn't want it at all. What he wants is Colonel Ryder's suitcase. Evidently you do too. I guess you'll have to draw straws for it. That all?"

"Oh, my lord." She was frowning. "This is an awful fix. But he doesn't know that you're bringing it—that you've got it."

"Sure he does."

"He can't. You've had no chance to tell him you found it."

"But he knows he sent *me* for it, therefore he knows it's on the way or soon will be."

She shook her head. "You never let up, do you?" Her tone implied that she would love to come out and play after she got her work done. "Of course he can't be sure. He couldn't have known I took it, and what if I had put it somewhere else? Which I would have done if I had used my brains, knowing you were around." She put her hand on my arm, not as for any purpose, just sort of involuntarily, as though it belonged there. She smiled at me as at a comrade. "I suppose you'd be surprised if I offered to give you ten thousand dollars for that carton—and what's in it—with the understanding that you forget all about it. Wouldn't you?"

I batted an eye. "I'd be simply dumbfounded."

"But you'd soon recover. And then what would you say?"

"Well, gosh." I patted her hand, which was still on my arm. "That would depend. If it was just conversation, I'd think of something appropriate to keep my end going, and start up the car and proceed. If you actually confronted me with the engravings, I'd have to see how I reacted."

She smiled. "It isn't likely I'd carry around a wad like that."

"Certainly not. So forget it." I started my hand for the dash.

But her hand held my arm. "Wait. You're too impulsive. It's a bona fide offer. Ten thousand."

"Cash?"

"Yes."

"When and where?"

"I think—" she hesitated. "I can have it in twenty-four hours. A little sooner. Tomorrow afternoon."

"And meanwhile, the carton?"

"The Day and Night Bank. In safekeeping for joint withdrawal only. We shake hands to pledge good faith."

I admired her visibly. It showed in my tone too. "Didn't I see you once walking the high wire at the circus? Maybe it was your sister. Looky. I suppose I could be had, but it isn't practical. Nero Wolfe would be sure to find out—he finds out everything in the long run—and he'd be sure to tell my poor old mother. If it wasn't for my mother I'd snap at it. I promised her once I'd never sell out for less than a million. The mortgage on the old farm happens to be a million even."

I started the engine and eased away from the curb into the traffic. She made no attempt to dangle the bait or put on another worm, and if she had I probably wouldn't have heard her. Several things had me guessing, and the one at the top of the list was the suitcase. Wolfe had said it was important, and here was this lovely innocent creature offering ten thousand bucks for it, when as far as I could see a reasonable OPA ceiling on it would have been twenty cents at the outside. It irritated me to be $9,999.80 out in my calculations, and since when I'm irritated I have a tendency to feed more gas, the remainder of the trip to Wolfe's place on 35th Street was a mere step.

It was only half an hour to dinner time, and I expected to find Wolfe in the kitchen supervising experiments, but he was hard at work at his desk in the office, rearranging field commanders probably, on his battle map of Russia. When we entered he kept right on.

Bruce said, "So this is Nero Wolfe's office," and looked around, at the leather chairs, the big globe, the shelves of books, the old-fashioned two-ton safe, the little bracket where he always had one orchid in bloom. I removed the cord from the carton, opened the flaps, got a grip on a section of the frame of the suitcase, pulled gently but firmly, got it out, and put it on a chair because the map was covering his desk. There were other items in the carton—papers and miscellany—but I stowed it over by the wall without disturbing them.

"Ah, you got it." Wolfe said, finally looking up. "Satisfactory. But evidently not unobserved. Did Miss Bruce come along to help you carry it?"

"No. She came because she can't bear to have it out of her sight. I went for it and it wasn't there. Gone. The corporal said nobody had taken anything. So since nobody had taken it, but it was gone, I figured that nobody couldn't be anybody but Sergeant Bruce. I had seen her in the anteroom packing things in a carton, and with the suitcase there on the floor only two steps from the door to the anteroom, and the corporal's back turned, it would have been a cinch for her and impossible for anyone else. Getting the address of her apartment and going there—two rooms, kitchenette and bath—I found the suitcase in the carton in the bedroom closet. Also in the closet was Lieutenant Lawson. Alive and well."

"The deuce he was." Wolfe leaned back and let his eyelids down a little. "Won't you be seated, Miss Bruce? No, that chair, if you don't mind."

The lovely innocent creature sat.

I resumed. "I didn't know whether Lawson was there as a cavalier or a porter or what. The conversation didn't light that up, except that she called him 'Ken darling.' So I left him and brought her and it. On the way here she made me a cash offer for the carton and contents—ten thousand dollars by tomorrow afternoon—and me erasing it from my mind. I think she'll pay more if you press her, but I didn't want to haggle because she had her hand on my arm. If you don't close with her, I'll give you a dime for it."

Wolfe grunted. "Her offer was for the carton and contents? What else is in it?"

"I haven't looked."

"Do so."

I picked it up and fished out the papers and miscellany, piling them on my desk. It was a thin crop—tennis racket, empty handbag, pair of stockings, a copy of *Is Germany Incurable?*, a jar of cream, other similar items. There was nothing among the papers to quicken my pulse—a copy of Army Regulations, four issues of *Yank*, a dozen or so G.I. postcards. I flipped the pages of the Regulations, and when a folded sheet of paper fluttered out I picked it up and unfolded it. It had typewriting on one side:

THE LAKE ISLE OF INNISFREE

I will arise and go now, and go to Innisfree,
And a small cabin build there, of clay and wattles
*   made;*
Nine bean rows will I have there, a hive for the
*   honey bee,*
And live alone in the bee-loud glade.

There was more of it. "This may be something," I told Wolfe. "Where's Innisfree?"

He was scowling at me. "What?"

"She writes poetry." I placed the sheet on the desk before him, stepping around so I could finish reading it. "She's going to Innisfree and build a cabin and start a victory garden and keep bees. Maybe there's more clues in it." I read on:

> And I shall have some peace there, for peace comes
>   dropping slow,
> Dropping from the veils of the morning to where
>   the cricket sings;
> There midnight's all a glimmer, and noon a
>   purple glow,
>   And evening full of the linnet's wings.
>
> I will arise and go now, for always night and day
> I hear lake water lapping with low sounds by the
>   shore;
> While I stand on the roadway, or on the pave-
>   ments gray,
>   I hear it in the deep heart's core.

"Defeatist," I declare. "Peace propaganda. Stop the war. And you notice—"

Wolfe cut me off. "Pfui. It was written fifty years ago, by Yeats." He wiggled a finger at the stack of junk on my desk. "Nothing in that?"

But I had perceived something which apparently he had missed. "Nevertheless," I insisted, "it reminds me of something." With my back to Sergeant Bruce, to obstruct her view I took from my pocket the piece of paper I had retrieved from the debris in Ryder's office, the anonymous letter Shattuck had got, unfolded it, and placed it on the desk beside the poem.

"And this wasn't written by Yeats, at least I don't think it was." As I talked I pointed to similarities of detail on the two sheets—the *c* below the line, the *a* off to the left, and others. "Of course it may be only an interesting coincidence, but it certainly stares you in the face."

"It is interesting," Wolfe conceded grudgingly. He was jealous because I had spotted it first. He got a magnifying glass from a drawer and examined the two sheets alternately. I shrugged and circled around to my chair and sat down. If he thought Bruce was too dumb to grasp the significance of a comparison of typescripts, time would teach him. But in a moment it became evident that he was doing it deliberately. He put the glass away and nodded at me approvingly.

"Your eye is still good, Archie. Unquestionably the same."

"Much obliged." I took the hint and fired another round. "If you're going to sic the dogs on it, a good place to start might be a portable Underwood I saw in her apartment."

He nodded again. "An excellent idea. This raises the point, regarding the generous offer she made you, what was she after, primarily? The suitcase, or this piece of typing, or both?"

"Or neither?" Sergeant Bruce suggested.

We both looked at her. She appeared, and sounded, totally unruffled and slightly amused.

"Neither?" Wolfe demanded.

She smiled at him. "Primarily, neither, Mr. Wolfe. Primarily, I was after you. The offer to Major Goodwin was just a little experiment, to test his loyalty to you. He mentioned a million as a joke, but you know quite well a million dollars is only a fraction of the total sum involved—or that will be involved. And certainly the services you are in a position to render will be well worth a fraction of the whole. Or, possibly, two fractions."

Chapter 5

About ten years ago a guy named Hallowell showed up at the office one evening with a canvas zipper bag containing a hundred and fifty thousand simoleons in fifties and centuries, with which he intended to short-circuit an electric current of two thousand volts which Wolfe was arranging for him to take sitting down, but that was only chicken feed compared to this. And, considering the secluded nature of the transaction, no income tax. A million dollars would buy four million bottles of the best beer.

Wolfe was leaning back in his chair, his eyes closed, his lips pushing out and in, out and in again. I was gazing straight at Bruce's face, impersonally, pondering the soundness of her assumption that Wolfe was worth a hundred times as much as me.

"I shouldn't think," the lovely innocent creature said in a matter-of-fact tone, "you would want to waste time on trivialities. Major Goodwin's guess happens to be correct—I typed that poem on my portable, from a book I had borrowed, because I liked it. And I suppose— Would you care to tell me what you were comparing it with?"

Wolfe muttered, without opening his eyes, "A letter Mr. Shattuck received."

She nodded. "Yes, that was typed on the same machine. And over thirty letters just like it, to different people in key positions. As you have doubtless already discovered, this affair is extremely complicated. It goes high, and it spreads wide. It really isn't worthy of you, Mr. Wolfe, to be wasting your talents on little details like that letter and Colonel Ryder's suitcase. We have been intending for some time to have a talk with you, awaiting the proper moment—and now of course you've forced us, with this suitcase business. We realize it will be very difficult to arrange. There will have to be mutual guarantees. Commitments of a kind that will make reconsideration impossible on either side. We're ready to discuss it whenever you are."

Wolfe's eyelids raised enough to show slits. "I like your dismissing the suitcase as a triviality, Miss Bruce. But if that's your whim— I suppose it would be futile for me to question you about it, or about this letter?"

"Such a waste of time," she protested.

"I presume it would be," he agreed. "But the suitcase is in my possession, and you admit that's what forced your hand. As for your offer to hire me, the difficulties seem almost insurmountable. For instance, you speak of 'we.' Much too vague, that is. I could discuss such a matter only with the principals, and how can they be disclosed to me, with the risk that as soon as I learn their identity I'll betray them?"

She shook her head, frowning at him. "You don't understand, Mr. Wolfe. The principals, as you call them, are above any risk of betrayal. As I said, this goes high. But even so, we have to use discretion, because we don't want—"

The phone ringing interrupted her. I got it at my

desk, and was informed that Washington was calling Nero Wolfe. I asked who was calling, and after a wait was told General Carpenter. I said to hold the wire, scribbled *Gen. Carp.* on my pad, and got up to hand it to Wolfe.

After a glance he turned it face down on his desk, and said politely to Bruce, "Mr. Goodwin will take you up and show you the orchids."

"If it's Lieutenant Lawson—" she began.

"Come on," I told her, "maybe you can worm it out of me."

It was hot in the plant rooms. I was sweating and she was a little flushed from the climb. Horstmann came trotting out, and I explained I was showing a guest around. I told her it was a little cooler in the potting-room, but she said no, she wanted to look at the plants, so I decided the best way to keep my mind off of the pleasing possibility of wringing her neck was to tell her the Latin names of the orchids. I did state that I would personally prefer to go to the potting-room, but couldn't, because if I left her alone she would swipe some of the plants to bribe people with. She flashed an appreciative glance at me and made her little noise, half gurgle and half chuckle, as if she did so enjoy my amusing remarks.

We were in the third room, where the germinating flasks were, when I heard the phone ringing in the potting-room, and went there to get it. I told it, "Goodwin speaking."

Wolfe's voice said, "Send Miss Bruce down here."

"You mean bring her down?"

"No. You are under the handicap of having sworn your oath as an officer in the Army. I am not. This may turn out to be a little delicate. I'd better talk with her privately."

Something more for me not to know. I sure was on the inside. I went and passed the word to Bruce and opened the doors for her through to the stairs. She descended. Going down one flight to my room, I couldn't see anything to interfere with rinsing the figure, so I stripped and stepped into the shower. Ordinarily I find that a good environment for sorting out my mind and fitting pieces together, but since in this case I was being stiff-armed clear off the field into the bleachers, I left the brain at ease and had a good time admiring my muscles and the hair on my chest. I was tying my good shoe laces when Fritz called up to say dinner was ready.

When I got downstairs, Wolfe was standing in the hall just outside the dining-room door. He waited till I approached, then turned and entered. We sat at the table.

"No company?" I inquired courteously. "Our new employer?"

"Miss Bruce went," he said.

Fritz came in with an earthenware pot on a serving platter, deposited it on the table in front of Wolfe, and lifted the lid. Steam and smell emerged and floated with the currents of air. Wolfe sniffed, leaned forward and sniffed again.

"Creole tripe," he said, "without the salt pork and pigs' feet. I'm anxious to see what you think." He inserted a serving spoon, releasing a fresh spurt of steam.

We had got started late, so it was along toward ten o'clock when we finished with coffee and went to the office. The stuff from the carton that I had piled on my desk was gone, and so was the carton. The map of Russia had been put away. The suitcase was still there on the chair. Instructed by Wolfe to put it in a safe place, I locked it in the closet, since it was too big for the safe. Wolfe was in his chair behind his desk, leaning back with his finger tips meeting at the spot where the ends of no one-yard tape measure would ever meet again. A book he was reading, *Under Cover*, by John Roy Carlson, was there on his desk, but he hadn't picked it up. I took a seat at my own desk and spoke.

"I'd hate to spoil anybody's fun," I said, "and I don't like to intrude a personal note, but it occurred to me some time ago that if Lawson is on the square and reports to his superiors that I called on Sergeant Bruce and kidnapped that carton, there'll be hell to pay."

Wolfe sighed. "You caught him hiding in a closet."

"Even so," I persisted.

"And surely he wouldn't do anything that might get Miss Bruce into trouble."

"No? What if he's on the square, and onto her, and playing her? Under orders from Ryder, or from Fife himself? Or Tinkham? You know how that outfit works. No matter who's behind you, always keep an eye over your shoulder."

Wolfe shook his head. "You know better than that, Archie. You have met Miss Bruce. Lieutenant Lawson lead that woman by the nose? Nonsense."

"I suppose," I said pointedly, "she must have explained to you where Lawson fits in. Naturally you wouldn't overlook a detail like that. Lawson Senior is one of the principals maybe?"

Wolfe frowned and sighed again. "Archie. Don't badger me. Confound it, I'm going to have to sit here and work, and I don't like to work after dinner. You're an Army officer, with the allegiances that involves, and this affair is too hot for you. I tell you, for instance, that Colonel Ryder was murdered, and I'm going to get the murderer. See where that puts you? What if one of your superior officers asks you a leading question? What if he orders you to make a report? As for Miss Bruce, I'm going to use her. I'm going to use Lawson. I'm going to use you. But right now, let me alone. Read a book. Look at pictures. Go to a movie."

His saying he was going to work meant he was going to sit with his eyes shut and heave a sigh three times an hour, and since if he got any bright ideas he was going to keep them to himself anyhow, I decided to make myself scarce. Also I had an outdoor errand, putting the car in the garage. I departed, performed the errand, and went for a walk. In the dim-out a late evening walk wasn't what it used to be, but since I was in no mood for pleasure, that was unimportant. Somewhere in the Fifties I resolved to make another stab at getting an overseas assignment. At home here, working in a uniform for Army G2 would have been okay, and working in my own clothes for Nero Wolfe would have been tolerable, but it seemed likely that trying to combine the two would sooner or later deprive me of the right to vote and then I could never run for President.

When I got back to the house on 35th Street, some time after eleven, because I was preoccupied with the future instead of the immediate present I wasn't aware of the presence of a taxicab discharging a passenger until the passenger crossed the sidewalk and mounted the stoop that was my own destination. By the time I had mounted the eight steps to his level he had his finger on the bell button. He heard me, and his head pivoted, and I recognized John Bell Shattuck.

"Allow me," I said, getting between him and the door. I inserted the key and turned it.

"Oh." He was peering at me in the dim light. "Major Goodwin. I'm seeing Mr. Wolfe."

"Does he know it?"

"Yes—I phoned him—"

"Okay." I let him in and closed the door. "I'll tell him you're here."

Wolfe's bellow came rolling through the open door to the office. "Archie! Bring him in!"

"Follow the sound waves," I told Shattuck. Which he did. I entered after him and crossed to my desk.

"You made a quick trip, sir," Wolfe rumbled. "Sit down. That chair's the best."

Shattuck, in dinner clothes with his tie off center and a spot of something on his shirt front, looked a little blowsy. He opened his mouth, then glanced at me and shut it, looked at Wolfe and opened it again.

"General Fife phoned me about Colonel Ryder. I was at that dinner and had to make a speech. I got away as soon as I could and phoned you." He glanced at me again. "If you'll excuse me, Major Goodwin, I think it would be better—"

I had crossed to my desk promptly and sat down because I was fully expecting Wolfe to shoo me out, and I wanted to register my opinion of his attitude in advance. But Shattuck put another face on it. He didn't merely suggest chasing me out, which Wolfe would have resented on principle, he tried to chase me himself without consulting Wolfe at all, which was intolerable.

"Major Goodwin," Wolfe told him, "is assigned here officially, serving me in a confidential capacity. Why, are you going to tell me something you don't want the Army to know?"

"Certainly not." Shattuck bristled. "I don't know anything I wouldn't want the Army to know."

"You don't?" Wolfe's brows went up. "Good heavens, I do. There are hundreds of things I wouldn't want anyone to know. You can't have as clean a slate as that, Mr. Shattuck, surely. But you want to tell me something about Colonel Ryder?"

"Not tell you. Ask you. Fife told me you were investigating and would report to him tomorrow. Have you got anywhere?"

"Well—some facts appear to be established. You remember that grenade, that pink thing, Colonel Ryder put in his desk drawer this morning—delivered to him by Major Goodwin. It exploded and killed Colonel Ryder. He must have removed it from the drawer, because there is evidence that it was on the desk top, or above it when it exploded. Also there are fragments of it all over the room."

I report what Wolfe said because I heard it and it registered somewhere in my mind but certainly not in the front of it. The front was occupied by something being registered not by hearing but by sight. My eye had just caught it. Behind Wolfe and off to the right—my right as I sat—was a picture on the wall, a painting on glass of the Washington Monument. (The picture, incidentally, was camouflage; it was actually a specially constructed cover for a panel through which you could view the office, practically all of it, from an alcove at the end of the hall next to the kitchen.) Just beyond the picture was a tier of shallow shelves holding various odds and ends, including mementos of cases we had worked on.

What had caught my eye was an object on the fourth shelf from the top that hadn't been there before, and to call it odd would have been putting it mildly, since it was a memento of the case then in progress and still unresolved. It was the grenade that had exploded and killed Ryder, standing there on its base, just as it had formerly stood on my chest of drawers upstairs.

Of course that was merely the first startling idea that popped into my mind when my eye hit it. But the idea that instantly took its place was startling enough—

the realization that it was another grenade exactly like the one Wolfe had ordered me to remove from the premises. I was positive it hadn't been there when I left two hours previously.

I may have been shocked into staring at it for two seconds, but no longer, knowing as I did that staring at other people's property wasn't polite. Apparently neither Wolfe nor Shattuck was aware that I was experiencing a major sensation, for they went right on talking. As I say, I heard them.

Shattuck was saying, "How and why did it explode? Have you reached any conclusions?"

"No," Wolfe said shortly. "It will be reported in the press as an accident, with no conjecture as to how it happened. General Fife says the safety pin on that grenade is jolt-proof, but expert opinions are by no means infallible. As for suicide, no mechanical difficulties certainly; he could simply have held the thing in his hand and pulled out the pin; but he would have had to want to. Did he? You might know about that; you were his son's godfather; you called him Harold; did he want to die?"

Shattuck's face twitched. After a moment he gulped. But his voice was clear and firm: "If he did I certainly didn't know it. The only thing is, his son had been killed. But a well man with a healthy mind can take a thing like that without committing suicide, and Harold Ryder was well and his mind was healthy. I hadn't seen a great deal of him lately, but I can say that."

Wolfe nodded. "Then the other alternative—that someone killed him. Since the grenade was used, it had to be procured from the desk drawer, presumably by one of us who saw Colonel Ryder put it there this morning. Six of us. That makes it a bit touchy."

"It sure does," Shattuck said grimly. "That's one reason I'm here. Got it from the drawer and then what?"

"I don't know. At that point the minutiae enter—entrances and exits, presences and absences. Opened the door, possibly, either door, pulled the pin, and tossed it in." Wolfe regarded him a moment inquiringly. "I take it, Mr. Shattuck, that this conversation is in confidence?"

"Of course it is. Entirely."

"Then I may say, tentatively, that a seventh person seems to be involved. Miss Bruce. Colonel Ryder's secretary."

"You mean that WAC in his anteroom?"

"Yes. I'm not prepared to give details, but it appears that Colonel Ryder had acquired certain information and had either drawn up a report or was getting ready to, and the result would have been disastrous for her."

Shattuck was frowning. "I don't like that."

"Indeed. You don't like it?"

"I mean I don't—" Shattuck stopped. The frown deepened. "I mean this," he said, in a harsh determined tone. "Since this is in confidence. I suspected, rightly or wrongly, that details regarding Captain Cross's death were being deliberately concealed and no real investigation was being made. I was satisfied on that score when I learned that you were handling it. You may ask then why am I not satisfied if you are in charge of the inquiry into Ryder's death? I am. But you may yourself be—misled. With all your talents, you may be off on a false scent. That's why I say I don't like that girl being dragged into it. I don't know her, know nothing about her, but it looks like a trick."

"Possibly," Wolfe conceded. "Have you any evidence that it is?"

"No."

"About those six people? Eliminate those here present, by courtesy. Those three people? Can you tell me anything about them?"

"No."

"Then I'm afraid we won't make any progress tonight." Wolfe glanced at the clock on the wall. He put his hands on the edge of the desk and pushed his chair back. "It's midnight. I assure you, sir, if tricks are being played on me I'm apt to find it out and return the compliment." He got to his feet. "I may have something more concrete for you by tomorrow. Say by tomorrow noon. Would it be convenient for you to drop in here at twelve noon? If I do have anything, I wouldn't care to announce it on the telephone."

"I think I can make it," Shattuck said, also standing. "I will make it. I have a reservation on the three o'clock plane for Washington."

"Good. Then I'll see you tomorrow."

I escorted the visitor to the front and let him out, closed the door and shot the night bolt, and returned to the office. I had supposed Wolfe was prepared to call it a day and go up to bed, but to my surprise he was back in his chair, and apparently, from the arrangement of his face, his mind was working.

I remarked rudely, "So you're going to use Shattuck too. For what? Is he it?"

"Archie. Be quiet."

"Yes, sir. Or is he Miss Bruce's principal and you're going to close the deal?"

No reply.

I went to the shelf and got the grenade, tossed it in the air, and caught it. I saw him shudder. That was something. "This," I said, "is Army property. So am I, as you remind me every hour on the hour. I don't ask where you got it, since you told me to be quiet. But I'll keep it in my room and return it to the Army in the morning."

"Confound you! Give me that thing."

"No, sir. I mean it. If I've got allegiances, as you say I have, I take this grenade to General Fife first thing in the morning, and I tell him—"

"Shut up!"

I stood and glared at him.

He glared back, as if something was almost more than he could bear, and he would leave it to me what.

Finally he said, "Archie. I submit to circumstances. So should you. And I'll make a concession to you. For instance, about that suitcase. Its metal frame is bent outward, in all directions. How could an explosion from anywhere on the outside of the suitcase, at whatever distance, near or far, bend its frame outward? It couldn't. Therefore the grenade was inside the suitcase when it exploded. The innumerable holes and tears in the leather made by the fragments confirm that. They are from the inside out."

I put the grenade on his desk.

"Therefore," he went on, "Colonel Ryder was murdered. The grenade couldn't possibly have exploded inside the suitcase by accident. Suicide, no. The man was not an idiot. He did not take the grenade from the desk drawer to kill himself with it, put it in the suitcase, and hold the lid open just enough to permit him to insert his hand to pull out the safety pin. That's the only way he could have done it, because the frame of the lid was bent outward too. Not suicide. Only one conclusion is tenable. It was a booby trap."

He picked up the grenade and indicated the thick

end of the pin. "You see that notch. I put the grenade in the suitcase, attach one end of a piece of string—even a narrow strip torn from a handkerchief would do— under that notch on the pin, pull the lid nearly shut, giving myself just room enough to work, attach the other end of the string to the lining of the lid at a front corner—probably with an office pin right there on the desk, a handy place to work—and close the lid. Two minutes would do it—not more than three. Whenever and wherever Colonel Ryder opened the suitcase, he would die. Since the lid was closed when the grenade exploded, probably he jerked the lid open to put something in and immediately snapped it shut again, without noticing the string. Of course, even if he had noticed it, that wouldn't have helped matters any."

I was considering the matter. When he stopped I nodded. "Okay," I agreed. "I'm right behind you. Next. Did Sergeant Bruce take it because she—"

"No," he said positively. He put the grenade in a drawer of his desk. "That's all."

"It's not even a start," I snorted.

"It's all for tonight." He stood up. "Come to my room at eight in the morning, when Fritz brings my breakfast. With your notebook. I'll have some instructions for you. It will be a busy day. We're going to set a booby trap—somewhat more complicated than that one."

Chapter 6

At 10:55 Tuesday morning I sat on a corner of my desk in Nero Wolfe's office, surveying the scene and the props. I had done the arranging myself, following instructions, but I had about as much idea what was going on as if I had been blindfolded at the bottom of a well.

Wolfe had been correct in one respect. At least so far it had been a busy day—for me. After an early breakfast I had gone to his room and been told what to do—not why or what for, just what. Then I had gone to Duncan Street and followed the program, without much time to spare, for General Fife didn't show up at his office until nearly ten o'clock. Returning home after I got through with him, I had arranged the props.

Not that they were elaborate or required much arranging; only three items, one on my desk and two on Wolfe's. One of the latter was a large envelope that had arrived in the morning mail. The address, to Nero Wolfe, was typed, and also typed was a line at the lower left-hand corner: *To be opened at six p.m. Tuesday, August 10th, if no word has been received from me.*

In the upper left-hand corner was the return:

Colonel Harold Ryder
633 Candlewood Street
New York City

The envelope, which, from the feel of it, contained several sheets of paper, was firmly sealed; hadn't been opened. It was on top of Wolfe's desk, a little to the right of the center, under a paperweight. The paperweight was the second item. It was the grenade, the twin of the one that killed Ryder.

And in the typing on the envelope the *c* was below the line, and the *a* was off to the left. It had been typed on the same machine as the poem Sergeant Bruce liked and the anonymous letter to Shattuck.

The item on my desk was a suitcase which belonged to me, my smallest one, a tan cowhide number that I used for short trips. The instructions had been to pack something in it—shirts, a few books, anything—and park it on my desk, and there it was.

Apparently that was the booby trap: the envelope, the grenade, and the suitcase. Whom it was supposed to catch, or how or when or why, I hadn't the faintest idea. In view of the further instructions I had received, it struck me as about the feeblest and foolishest effort to bait a murderer that the mind of man had ever conceived. I relieved my emotions by making a few audible remarks that I could have picked up in barracks if I had ever been in barracks, left the scene and went up three flights to the roof, found Wolfe in the potting-room arranging sphagnum, and told him, "All set."

He inquired without interrupting his labors, "The articles in the office?"

"Yep."

"You asked them to be punctual?"

"I did. Lawson at 11:15, Tinkham at 11:30, Fife at 11:45. You invited Shattuck and Bruce yourself."

"Fritz? The panel?"

"I said," I told him icily, "all set. For what, God knows."

"Now Archie," he murmured, pulling moss apart. "It's barely possible that I'm nervous. This thing is ticklish. If it doesn't work we may never get him. By the way—get Mr. Cramer on the phone."

When I did so, using the phone there on the bench, Wolfe put on a show. After telling me he was nervous because it was so ticklish, he bulled it like this with Cramer:

"Good morning, sir. About that affair downtown. I promised to phone you my opinion today. It was premeditated murder. That's all I can tell you now, but developments may be expected shortly. No, sir, you will do nothing of the sort. You'll only be making a fool of yourself. How can you, until I've explained it to you? If you come here now, you will not be admitted. I expect to phone you later in the day to tell you who the murderer is and where to go for him. Certainly not! No, sir."

He replaced the receiver. "Pfui," he muttered, and went back to the sphagnum.

"Cramer will be a little petulant if it doesn't work," I observed.

His shoulders lifted, just perceptibly, and dropped again. "Now it will have to work. What time is it?"

"Eight after eleven."

"Get down to the alcove. Lieutenant Lawson might be early."

I departed.

I can't remember that I ever felt sillier than I did during the hour that followed. The operation was simple. I was to station myself in the alcove at the end of the hall, by the panel which permitted a view of the office. As each visitor arrived, Fritz was to tell him that Wolfe would be down in ten minutes, and escort him to the office and close the office door. I was to observe his actions while he waited in the office. I was to do nothing about it unless he monkeyed with one or more of the props. If he merely looked at them, picked them up and put them down again, okay; if he did something more drastic, I was to report to Wolfe on the phone in the kitchen. Otherwise I stayed put.

Five minutes before the time scheduled for the next visitor to arrive, Fritz was to go for the incumbent in the office, tell him Wolfe wanted him to come up to the plant rooms, and escort him there, thus vacating the office for the next one. If one of the victims arrived ahead of time, Fritz was to put him in the front room until the office was ready for him.

There was nothing wrong with that, and it worked as smooth as silk. Lawson came at 11:13. Tinkham came at 11:32. Fife came at 11:50. Shattuck came at 12:08. Sergeant Bruce came at 12:23. Fritz's shuttle service worked perfectly, up to a certain point, which I'm coming to.

As I say, I never felt sillier than I did glued to that panel, watching them come and go. Granted that one of them was a murderer, what the hell did Wolfe expect him to do? Grab the envelope and run? Kill himself with the grenade? Give an encore of his performance the day before with the grenade and the suitcase? For my money, the murderer wouldn't do any of these things, or anything resembling them, if he had the brains God gave geese.

He didn't do any of them, if he was among those present.

Lawson, first to arrive, left alone in the office by

Fritz, stood and looked the place over, approached the desk, cocked his head at the envelope and grenade, sat down, and didn't move again until Fritz came for him.

Tinkham showed more interest. He spotted the props immediately. When Fritz left and shut the door, Tinkham turned to look at the door, started to cross to it, changed his mind and returned to the desk, picked up first the grenade, then the envelope, and inspected them. He kept glancing at the door. If he was trying to make up his mind what to do, he never got that far, for he had the envelope in his hand giving it a third inspection, when the door opened and Fritz entered. Tinkham dropped the envelope on the desk, without, as far as I could see, skipping a heartbeat. When Fritz had left with him I went in and arranged things as before and returned to my post.

Fife was a washout. It didn't seem possible, but I swear that as far as I could tell he never saw them at all.

Shattuck was the only one that seemed to notice the suitcase, but he noticed everything. He didn't touch; he just looked. He went to the desk and looked there; stared at the envelope and grenade. Then he went to my desk and looked there. After that he sort of took in all the surroundings, then did the two desks again. But he didn't touch a thing.

I was looking forward to the last and as far as I was concerned least, Sergeant Bruce. I doubt if anything she might have done would have surprised me, from pulling the pin of the grenade and tossing it out the window to opening the suitcase and copping one of my shirts. But actually, I admit she did surprise me. She wasn't in the office more than twenty seconds all together, after Fritz left and closed the door. She went and got the grenade and the envelope, and, without bothering to give them a look, put them in a drawer of

Wolfe's desk and shut the drawer, and beat it. Out she popped. If I had wanted to stop her I would have had to jump. I heard her going down the hall and the front door closing. I stepped around the corner, and no sergeant. She had skedaddled.

At that point I gave up entirely. I went to the office, to the phone on my desk, buzzed the plant rooms, and told Wolfe what had happened. Then, still following instructions, I retired to the kitchen. I wasn't supposed to show up in the office until after they had come down from the plant rooms. Why? As far as I knew, because. Evidently they were in no hurry. I had finished two bananas and a glass of milk before I heard the elevator complaining. After hearing their voices in the hall I gave them time to get in the office and solve the seating problem. Then I joined them.

It didn't strike me as an atmosphere of jollity, as I circled around their chairs to reach mine at my desk. I would have been perfectly willing to salute my superior officers, but their attitudes didn't seem to call for it. None of them was in handcuffs or even had his insignia ripped off, so as far as I could see the booby trap was a turkey. The closest chair to mine was Shattuck's, and beyond him was Tinkham. Fife was in the big one at the other end of Wolfe's desk. Lawson was to his right and back of him.

Wolfe, having got himself comfortably adjusted, sighed clear to the bottom. "Now," he said in a tone of satisfaction, "we can proceed. I thank you gentlemen again for your patience. I hope you'll agree with me, when I've explained, that it was worth it. It was the only way that occurred to me of learning whether one of you murdered Colonel Ryder, or Miss Bruce did."

"Murder?" Fife was scowling at him. "Goodwin told me you didn't know—"

"If you please, General." Wolfe was curt. "This will take all day if you start heckling. What Major Goodwin told you, and Colonel Tinkham and Lieutenant Lawson, was that I wanted to see you at my office, privately, that I was still undecided as to the manner of Colonel Ryder's death, that I had learned that Miss Bruce was involved on account of a report being prepared by Colonel Ryder which would have meant her ruin, and that I had received a sealed communication from Colonel Ryder, mailed yesterday, which I wished to open in your presence."

"But now you say—"

"General. Please." Wolfe's eyes swept the circle. "I can now tell you that I devised an experiment. I arranged for you to arrive here at fifteen-minute intervals, and to be left alone in this office. On the desk where you couldn't fail to see it was an envelope addressed to me, with Colonel Ryder's return address, his home address, and the inscription, *To be opened at six p.m. Tuesday, August 10th, if no word has been received from me.* Incidentally, that envelope was a fake. I had it prepared and mailed last evening."

"I wondered about that," Colonel Tinkham said dryly. "It was postmarked eleven p.m. Ryder had been dead seven hours."

"Irrelevant," Wolfe snapped. "That could have been accounted for in a dozen ways. On the envelope I placed a grenade like the one that killed Colonel Ryder. I asked General Carpenter for it on the phone last evening, and he sent it by messenger on a plane. The experiment was to leave each of you in here alone for ten minutes, with those objects on the desk, and see what would happen. After each of you left, Fritz came in to inspect—especially to learn if the envelope had been tampered with. That may seem a little crude. But

consider: consider the state of mind of the murderer.
Could he stay in here alone for ten minutes, with that
envelope staring him in the face, and do nothing about
it? Make no effort whatever to learn what was in it?
Impossible. Absolutely impossible!"

Fife snorted. "I never saw the damn thing. I don't
see it now." He was regarding Wolfe as anything but a
valued associate. "And you had the gall, by God, to put
me on your list!"

"It impresses me," Tinkham said coldly, "as kindergarten stuff."

"Ah, Colonel," Wolfe wiggled a finger at him, "but it
worked!" He wiggled the finger at the desk. "As General Fife remarked, he doesn't see it now. It's gone."

They all goggled at him. Then, as the implication
soaked in, they looked at one another. Currents of
startled inquiry, uneasiness, distrust, darted from one
pair of eyes to another, here and there, in all directions,
crossing, meeting.

Fife barked at Wolfe, "What the hell are you talking
about? What are you insinuating?"

"Nothing," Wolfe said quietly. "I'm merely reporting. I know you gentlemen are on edge, but even so you
might let me finish. As I said, Fritz entered to look
things over after each of you had been in here ten
minutes. And all of you passed the test admirably.
Lawson, Tinkham, Fife, Shattuck. But there was another. The last to come was Miss Bruce. She too had her
allotted ten minutes. But, gentlemen, she remained for
only seven of them! The keyhole of the kitchen door
commands a view of the hall. After seven minutes Fritz
saw Miss Bruce emerge from the office and depart by
the front door. He came in here—and both the envelope
and the grenade were gone! Why she took the grenade

I don't know, unless for the purpose of hurling it through the window at me."

They all glanced at the window, and I did too, to make it unanimous.

Fife was on his feet. "I want to use that phone."

Wolfe shook his head. "It requires a little discussion, General. For one thing, we can't afford to make enemies of the police. For another, they are already attending to Miss Bruce. I arranged with Inspector Cramer to post men outside, to follow any of you, including Miss Bruce, who left the house before one o'clock. For still another, General Carpenter phoned me from Washington last evening and gave me some special instructions. As I said, he sent me that grenade. And with it, the instructions in writing. So if you'll bear with me a little longer—"

Fife sat down.

"I do not state," Wolfe said, "that Miss Bruce murdered Colonel Ryder. She has the appearance of a resourceful and determined woman, but we certainly haven't enough evidence to charge her with murder. Why she stayed in here seven minutes, instead of seizing the envelope as soon as she saw it and leaving with it, I don't know. She may have been coolheaded enough to open it and examine the contents, but that doesn't seem likely, since all it contained was blank sheets of paper. At any rate, we can now start to work on her, and whether her wrongdoing went to the length of murder or not, she'll pay for whatever she did." Wolfe frowned. "I admit I don't like her having that grenade. I didn't foresee that. If she gets in a corner and kills someone with it—" He shrugged. "Archie, you'd better phone Mr. Cramer and tell him to warn his men—but first, where's that letter from General Carpenter? Have you got it in your desk?"

It was just as I opened my mouth to answer him that I realized what he was doing. This was the booby trap.

"I don't think so," I said. "I think you took it. I'll look." I pulled a drawer of my desk open. I would have given a month's pay to be able to watch their faces, but I knew that was Wolfe's part of it and went on with mine. I shut the drawer and opened another one. "Not here." I opened a third drawer and closed it.

Wolfe, leaning back with his arms folded, said testily, "Try mine."

I went around to the side of his desk and did so. The middle drawer; the three on the left; the four on the right. I was about to mutter something about trying the files when Wolfe spoke.

"Confound it, I remember! I put it back in the suitcase. Get it."

I returned to my desk. Just as my fingers were reaching for the catches of the suitcase Wolfe's voice snapped like a whip: "Mr. Shattuck! What's the matter?"

"Matter? Nothing," Shattuck's reply came, but it wasn't much like his voice.

I wheeled to look at him. His hands were grasping the arms of his chair, his jaw was clamped, and his eyes glittered with what seemed to be, from my distance, half fear and half fight.

"It's adrenaline," Wolfe told him. "You can't control it. Perhaps you would have done better if you were a brave man, but obviously you're a coward." He reached down and pulled a drawer open, and his hand came up holding the grenade. "See, here it is. Just to reassure you. Calm yourself. Miss Bruce didn't set a trap with it in one of the drawers, or in that suitcase, as you did yesterday in Colonel Ryder's suitcase." He put the grenade on his desk.

"Good God," Fife said.

Lawson got up and stood there in front of his chair, stiff and erect as at attention.

Tinkham, who had been staring at Wolfe, transferred the stare to Shattuck, and stroked his mustache.

Shattuck neither moved nor spoke. He hadn't recovered control, and he was waiting till he did. He may not have been brave, but he had a good set of brakes.

Wolfe rose to his feet. "General," he said to Fife, "I'm afraid you're out of this. Mr. Shattuck is not in the Army, so it's for the civil authorities after all. I want him where he'll feel free to talk, so he and I are going for a little ride in my car. Major Goodwin will drive us. If you gentlemen are thirsty, Fritz will serve you." He turned. "Mr. Shattuck. You can tell me to go to the devil. You can run to your lawyers. You can, for the moment, do whatever you please. But I strongly advise you, if you know me at all, and from what you said yesterday you seem to have heard my name, to accept my invitation to talk it over with me."

Chapter 7

To Van Cortlandt Park," Wolfe directed me from the rear seat.

If and when I write a book called *Interesting Trips I Have Taken*, that one will be the first on the list.

I was behind the wheel. I was violating Regulations by having three buttons on my jacket unfastened, for quick and easy access to the gun in my shoulder holster. That was on my own initiative. John Bell Shattuck was in front beside me, and had not been frisked. In the back was Wolfe, alone, making a more comical picture than usual, for the hand that was not gripping the strap at the side was gripping something else: the grenade. Whether he had brought it along for protection, or just to get it out of the house, I didn't know; but he sure was hanging on to it. And why Van Cortlandt Park? He had never been anywhere near the place.

I headed for the 47th Street entrance to the West Side Highway.

"It was sensible for you to come along without protest, Mr. Shattuck," Wolfe rumbled.

"I'm a sensible man," Shattuck said. Apparently he was in running order again. There was no adrenaline in his voice. He had twisted around on the seat to be able to face Wolfe. "Whatever you're up to—I don't know what you're driving at. To accuse me of killing Harold Ryder was absolutely ridiculous, and you couldn't possibly have been serious. But you said it before four witnesses. I came with you—away from them—because I'm willing to give you a chance to explain—if you can. But it will have to be damned good."

"I'll make it as good as I can," Wolfe told him. We crossed the 42nd Street car tracks. "Archie. Go slower."

"Yes, sir."

"I'll try to keep to the essentials," Wolfe said. "If you want a point elaborated, say so. First, I confess that most of what I told you and the others was a pack of lies."

"Ah," Shattuck said. "But you haul me off alone to admit it. I expect you to justify that. Let's hear you."

"I'll specify—" Wolfe grunted as we hit a little bump. "—a few of the lies. I was not undecided as to the manner of Colonel Ryder's death. One look at the remains of his suitcase told the story—by the way, I have it in my office. I got no letter of instructions from General Carpenter, though I did talk with him on the phone. He's coming to New York this afternoon and will dine with me this evening. But most of the lies concerned Miss Bruce. Practically everything I said about her was untrue. She was under no suspicion. Colonel Ryder was preparing no report that could have injured her. I had not arranged with the police to follow her when she left my house. The truth is, Miss Bruce is a confidential assistant of General Carpenter, reporting directly to him. He told me last evening that she's worth any two men on his staff. I doubt that, but she did show some intelligence about the suitcase. Seeing it only from a distance of several feet, from the door of the anteroom, she saw the significance of its condition."

"What the devil was the significance of its condition?" Shattuck demanded.

"Now, now," Wolfe reproached him. "I beg you, none of those transparent implications of innocence. Miss Bruce was also clever enough to get the suitcase out of there, to show to General Carpenter. He had sent her to New York because of indications that someone in that unit was involved in the suspected transactions regarding industrial secrets. It was she who typed that anonymous letter to you—incidentally, you shouldn't have let it scare you like that. No one had the slightest suspicion of you. The same letter was sent to some thirty people—key people in legislative and administrative positions. They were merely fishing. It was different with Colonel Ryder. There was no proof, but he was under observation, and that's why Miss Bruce was assigned to his office from Washington. He may have suspected something of the sort, and that was a factor in his decision to go to General Carpenter and make a clean breast of it. Another—"

"By God!" Shattuck cut in. "That's dirty! That's lousy! If you want to make damn fool accusations about me, and stand the consequences, that's all right, I'm here, and I can take care of myself, and I will. But Harold's dead. To start a dirty lie like that about a dead man—"

"Stop it," Wolfe said curtly. "You'll have me thinking you're not only a coward but a fool. To try to impress me with that rubbish! You know quite well why you came and got in this car with me: to find out how much I know. Then let me talk. Speak only if you want to say something. Where was I? Oh, Miss Bruce. That will do for her. I may mention that Lieutenant

Lawson is also on special assignment from General Carpenter, as a sort of errand boy for Miss Bruce. In that capacity he may possibly be satisfactory. I wouldn't be telling you these things, Army secrets in a way, if there were any chance of your passing them on. But there's no risk, since in an hour from now, less than that I should say, you won't be alive."

Shattuck stared at him, speechless.

We were rolling along the West Side Highway. I was myself sufficiently startled to look aside at Shattuck, and returned to my driving just in time to jerk away from kissing the curb.

"Are you crazy?" Shattuck found his voice to ask.

"No, sir," Wolfe said. "I did state an overwhelming probability as a certainty. We all do that."

"I won't be alive? An hour from now?" Shattuck laughed, and it wasn't very hollow at that. "This is incredible. I suppose you're going to threaten to blow me to pieces with that grenade unless I sign a confession to anything you tell me to. Absolutely unbelievable!"

"Not like that. The grenade, yes. I brought it along for you to kill yourself with."

"By God—you *are* crazy!"

Wolfe shook his head. "Don't shout at me. Keep your wits. You're going to need them. Archie, where are you going?"

"Leaving the highway," I told him, "for the park entrance. Then what?"

"Secluded roads in the park."

"Yes, sir." We rolled on down the incline.

"The reason you shouted," Wolfe went on to Shattuck, "was because the first glimmer of a fact darted into your brain—the fact that you are fighting for your life. That was a mean trick I played you in my office.

You had seen the grenade on my desk. You were told that a person who thought I was endangering her safety had been in there alone for seven minutes, had departed, and the grenade had disappeared. The most vivid impression your mind held at that moment was the memory of what you yourself had done the day before with a grenade like that one. When Major Goodwin began pulling drawers open—the grenade trap, just like the one you had set, *might* have been in any of them—control of your involuntary processes was out of the question. When I told him to open the suitcase—it's a pity you couldn't have seen yourself. It was magnificent—better, really, than if you had leaped screaming to your feet and fled from the room.

"Archie, confound it, can't you see a hole?

"What you want, of course, is to learn how much I know. How much General Carpenter knows. I'm not going to tell you. You got in this car with me to match your wits against mine. Abandon the attempt. If we met on equal terms, there's no telling what the score would be, but we don't. I am free and safe; you are a doomed man. You're cornered, with no space to maneuver."

"I'm letting you talk," Shattuck said. "You're talking drivel."

We entered Van Cortlandt Park.

Wolfe ignored his remark. "A crook is not always a fool," Wolfe said. "As you know, Mr. Shattuck, there are men in high places in public life, even as high as yours, who are venal, dishonest and betrayers of trust, and who yet will die peacefully in their beds, surrounded with tokens of respect, their chief regret being that they will be unable to read the glowing obituaries the following day. You might have been one of them. From the tremendous backlog of credit for services performed which you were piling up among wealthy and influential persons, by these crooked operations you were supervising and protecting from attack, you might even have succeeded in reaching the limit of your ambition.

"But you had bad luck. You encountered me. I have two things. First, I have ingenuity. I used it today, with the result that you are here with me now. Second, I have pertinacity. I have decided that the simplest way out of this business is for you to die. I am counting on you to agree with me. If you don't, if you try to fight it out, try to go back to life, you're lost. There is not now sufficient evidence to convict you of the murder of Colonel Ryder. Perhaps there never will be; but there will be enough to indict you and put you on trial. I'll see to that. If you are acquitted, I shall only have begun. I shall never stop. There is the murder of Captain Cross. There are all the hidden transactions and convolutions of your traffic in the industrial secrets entrusted to our Army to help fight the war.

"Now that I know who you are and know where to look, how long will it take me to get enough to impeach you, drag you into court, condemn you? A week? A month? A year? What about your associates, when they see the lightning about to strike and smash you? Colonel Ryder will never testify against you, you saw to that, but there are others. How about them, Mr. Shattuck? Can you trust them further than you could trust your old friend Ryder when we get to them and they are ready to break? You can't kill all of them, you know."

Shattuck was no longer looking at Wolfe. His body was still twisted around on the seat, but from the corner of my eye I could see that his gaze was aimed straight past my chin, on through the open window.

"Stop the car, Archie," Wolfe said.

I swerved to the grassy shoulder and stopped. We were on one of the secondary roads in the higher section of the park, and, on a weekday, there wasn't a soul in sight. To the left was woods, sloping down; to the right was a stretch of meadow with scattered trees, gently rising. All it needed was a herd of cows to make it a remote spot in Vermont.

"Is this a dead-end road?" Wolfe asked.

"No," I told him, "it goes on over the hill and meets the north drive going east."

"Then get out, please." I did so. Wolfe handed me the grenade. "Take this thing." He pointed up the rise, at right angles to the road, to a big tree in the meadow. "Put it on the ground there at the base of that tree. Next to the trunk."

"Just lay it on the ground?"

"Yes."

I obeyed. On my way across the meadow, a good hundred yards, and back again, I spent the time making book. I finally settled on even money. That may sound like shading it in Wolfe's favor, but I was right there listening to it and seeing them. Wolfe's voice alone was half of it. It was hard, dry, assured. It made it hard to believe that anything it said would happen, wouldn't happen. The other half was the way Shattuck looked. Now that I wasn't driving and could take him in, I realized that the jolt he had got in the office, utterly unexpected, had given him a shock that he hadn't even begun to recover from. He was flat, taking the count, and Wolfe was doing the counting. When I reached the car Wolfe was saying:

"If so, you're mistaken. I would prefer to fight it out with you, and so would General Carpenter. You don't stand a chance. If you're not put to death by the people of the state of New York, you're done for anyhow. At a minimum, irremediable disgrace, the ruin of your career. But I don't pretend that I brought you here, to this, as a favor to you. We would prefer to fight it out with you, but we're working for our country, and our country is at war. To break a scandal like this, at this time, would do enormous damage. If it can possibly be avoided, it should be. I say that not to affect your decision, for I know it wouldn't, but to explain why I took the trouble to bring you here."

I opened the front door on Shattuck's side, leaned against it to keep it from swinging shut, and told Wolfe, "There's a flat rock there right near the tree. I put it on that."

Shattuck looked at me as if he was going to say something, but nothing came out. He wet his lips with his tongue, kept on looking at me, and then wet his lips again.

Wolfe said harshly, "Get out of the car, Mr. Shattuck. It isn't a long walk—not much more than down that corridor to Colonel Ryder's office and back again. Thirty or forty seconds, that's all. We'll wait here. It will be an accident. I promise you that. The obituaries will be superb. All that any outstanding public figure could ask."

Shattuck slowly turned to him. "You can't expect me—" He didn't have much voice, and in a moment he tried again. "You can't expect me to—" He tried to swallow, and it wouldn't work.

"Help him out, Archie."

I took his elbow, and he came. His foot slipped off the running board, and I held him up, and led him away a couple of paces on the grass.

"He's all right," Wolfe said. "Come and get in."

I climbed in the car and slammed the door and slid

across behind the wheel. Wolfe spoke through his open window.

"If you change your mind, Mr. Shattuck, come back to the road, and we'll take you back to town, and the fight will be on. I advise against it, but I doubt if my advice is needed. You're a coward, Mr. Shattuck. I've had wide experience, and I've never known of a more cowardly murder than the murder of Colonel Ryder. Hang on to that as your bulwark. Say to yourself as you cross the meadow, 'I'm a coward. I'm a coward and a murderer.' That will carry you through, right to the end. You need something to take you that hundred yards, and since it can't be courage, let it be your integrity, your deep inner necessity, as a coward. And this too, this knowledge, if you come back, you're coming back to us—to me. I'll be waiting."

Wolfe stopped, because Shattuck was moving. He moved slowly, down the little incline into the drainage ditch, and then up the other side. In a few paces he began to go faster, and he kept on a straight line, straight for the tree. About halfway there his foot caught on something and he nearly fell, but then he was upright again and going faster.

Wolfe muttered at me, "Start the car. Go ahead. Slowly."

I thought that was a mistake. Shattuck was sure to hear the sound of the engine, and there was no telling what that would do to him. But I did as I was told, as quietly as possible. I eased the car back onto the road and let it crawl uphill. It covered 100 yards, 200.

Wolfe's voice came. "Stop."

I shifted to neutral, set the hand brake, let the engine run, and turned in my seat to look back across the meadow. I caught one last brief glimpse of John Bell

Shattuck, kneeling there by the tree, his torso bent over, and then—

Nothing got to us but the sound, and that wasn't anything like as loud as I expected. I could see nothing in the air but the cloud of dust. But a moment later, four seconds maybe, there was a soft rustling noise as particles fell into the grass over a wide area; a noise like the big scattered raindrops that start a summer shower.

"Go ahead," Wolfe said curtly. "Get to a telephone. Confound it, I've got to speak to Inspector Cramer."

Chapter 8

For dinner we had clams, frog legs, roast duck Mr. Richards, roasted corn on the cob, green salad, blackberry pie, cheese, and coffee. I sat across from Wolfe. On my right was General Carpenter. On my left was Sergeant Bruce. Obviously Wolfe had known Carpenter was going to bring her along, since the table was set for four before they arrived, but he hadn't mentioned it to me. She ate like a sergeant, if not in manner, anyhow in quantity. We all did.

In the office, after the meal, I lighted cigarettes for her and me. Carpenter, in the red leather chair that John Bell Shattuck had occupied the evening before, filled a pipe and lighted it, crossed his legs, and puffed. Wolfe, disposed for comfort on his throne behind his desk, took it like a man. He hated pipes, but the expression on his face said plainly, at least to me, this is war and one must not shrink from the hardships.

"I still don't understand," Carpenter said, "why Shattuck exposed his flanks like that."

Wolfe sighed with contentment. "Well," he murmured, "he didn't think he was. First, he underrated me. Second, he grossly overrated himself. That's an occupational disease of those in the seats of the mighty.

Third, that anonymous letter got him flustered. That was close to a stroke of genius, sending those letters out promiscuously."

Carpenter nodded. "Dorothy's idea. Miss Bruce."

I thought to myself, *Huh. "Dorothy." "Ken darling." She sure does get on a sociable basis.*

"She appears to have some intelligence," Wolfe conceded. "Nevertheless, she is a jenny ass. She hasn't told you, of course, that she undertook to test my integrity and Major Goodwin's. She offered to buy me for a million dollars. Since she has streaks of brilliance, use her by all means, but I think you should know that she also has a streak of imbecility. It was the most transparent springe ever devised by a female brain."

"To you, perhaps." Carpenter was smiling. "But I had suggested it to her. I told her to try you out if an opportunity came. With the interests and the sums involved, I was even keeping an eye on myself. And while I was aware of your talents—"

Wolfe grimaced. "Bah." He waved it away, from the wrist. "You might at least have shown a little ingenuity in concealing the noose. As for Shattuck, he couldn't help himself. Probably he had already had a hint that Ryder was about to crumple up."

"I still don't understand Ryder. I would have sworn he was as sound as they come, but he had a rotten spot."

"Not necessarily," Wolfe disagreed. "Possibly only a vulnerable one. No telling what. They were old friends, and who is so apt to know the secret word, the hidden threat, that will paralyze a man into helplessness, as an old friend? But Ryder got two shocks, simultaneously, that caused the threat, whatever it was, to lose its power. His beloved only son got killed in battle, and one of his men, Captain Cross, was murdered. The first altered all his values; and connivance at murder was not in his contract. He decided to go to you and let it out, and he informed Shattuck of his decision, not privately—he didn't want to discuss it or argue about it—but publicly, irrevocably, before witnesses. That's what it amounted to."

"What a fix for a man," Carpenter muttered.

"Yes. Also a fix for Shattuck. He was done for too. After that he really had no choice, and circumstances made it, if not easy for him, at least not too difficult. Returning after lunching with General Fife, all he had to do was get three or four minutes alone in Ryder's office, and doubtless he didn't find that very hard to manage. Then, I suppose, he left for some appointment. Men of his prominence always have appointments. You asked me before dinner if he killed Captain Cross too. As a conjecture, yes. If you're going to complete the file on it, find out if he was in New York last Wednesday evening, and follow the trial." Wolfe shrugged. "He's dead."

Carpenter nodded. He was gazing at Wolfe with a certain expression, an expression I had often seen on the faces of people sitting in that chair looking at Wolfe. It reminded me of what so many out-of-town folks say about New York: that they love to visit the place, but you couldn't pay them to live there. Me, I live there.

Carpenter said, "What put you onto him?"

"I've already told you. His reaction, here, when Major Goodwin opened drawers and started to open the suitcase. Until then, I didn't know. It might have been Fife, or Tinkham, or even Lawson. By the way," Wolfe glanced at the clock, "they'll be here in twenty minutes. I'll explain to them about Miss Bruce, tell them I was merely using her, since you don't want her real status revealed. But the instructions about Shattuck are to be an order from you. I promised him it would be an accident, and I'm holding to that line with the police, though Inspector Cramer knows better. He knows—he has had contacts with me before, over a period of years. That scene here today—what I said to Shattuck—is for no open record or general conversation."

"I'll see to that," Carpenter agreed. "With the understanding, of course, that it is not to impede future operations. We'll never get anyone who was concerned in it, but at least we'll stop it, and we'll stop them. I'm wondering—We might have broken Shattuck's back, we just might—if we still had him."

"Pfui." Wolfe was complacent. "If he had had real stuff in him, if he had stuck it out and fought it out, we would have got nowhere. Convict him of murder? Nonsense. As for the rest, the battalions of wealth, legal talent and political power that would have lined up behind him— He could have thumbed his nose at us." Wolfe sighed. "But he had annoyed me. He had challenged me. He came here last evening to warn me not to allow anyone to play tricks on me! So, knowing myself, I knew I'd never be able to let go of him, and I couldn't afford it. As you know, I take no pay for this government work, and it leaves me little time for my private detective business. I simply couldn't afford to spend the next three years, or five or ten, attending to Mr. Shattuck, or trying to."

Carpenter gazed at Wolfe, puffing on his pipe. After about six pulls he realized he was out, and reached in his pocket for a match.

I dived into the opening.

"Major Goodwin," I said, "requests permission to speak to General Carpenter."

Carpenter frowned at me. "You'd never make a soldier. You're too damn fresh. What do you want?"

"A suggestion, sir. I understand that General Fife

and Colonel Tinkham are to be kept in ignorance of what Sergeant Bruce is: the brains of G2, apparently. So I should think they would be startled by her presence here and maybe suspect she is not a simple little WAC. So I just whispered to her to ask if she likes to dance, and she whispered back that she does. I respectfully suggest—"

"Go on, go on, get out of here, both of you. It's a good idea at that, isn't it, Dorothy?"

She nodded. "That's why I told him I like to dance."

Momentarily, I let it go. But after we had left the house and walked to the corner and flagged a taxi and she had got in, I spoke to her through the open door.

"Let's start from scratch. He can take you to Eleventh Street, or he can take us uptown. Do you like to dance or don't you?"

"Yes," she said.

"Then your telling the boss that you told me you like to dance because it would be for the good of your country and help win the war for you to leave there, that was a lie?"

"Yes."

"Swell. Now all the familiarity. 'Ken darling.' 'Dorothy' from the boss. Did you sit on their laps when you were a baby, or is it a recently formed habit?"

She chuckled and gurgled, or whatever that noise was. "That," she said, "is nothing but congenital friendly exuberance. Also I feel rather protective about them. I feel that way, more or less, about lots of men— those I don't dislike. They're so darned dumb."

I grinned at her. "Fifty years from now I'll remind you of that, and you'll claim you never said it." I got in the cab. "For myself I don't care, but my colleagues, one billion human males, are counting on me."

I told the driver, "Flamingo Club."

The World of
Rex Stout

Now, for the first time ever, enjoy a peek into the life of Nero Wolfe's creator, Rex Stout, courtesy of the Stout Estate. Pulled from Rex Stout's own archives, here are rarely seen, some never-before-published memorabilia. Each title in "The Rex Stout Library" will offer an exclusive look into the life of the man who gave Nero Wolfe life.

Not Quite Dead Enough

The original dust jacket from *Not Quite Dead Enough*, published September 7, 1944. The trim size of the book—an unusual 5 x 7½ inches—was smaller because, according to the copyright page:

WAR EDITION

Complete text—reduced size in accordance with paper conservation orders of the War Production Board.

NOT QUITE DEAD ENOUGH

A NERO WOLFE
DOUBLE MYSTERY

Rex Stout